The Kidnappers

a mystery

W9-CLF-421

Books by Willo Davis Roberts

The View from the Cherry Tree
Don't Hurt Laurie!
More Minden Curses
The Girl with the Silver Eyes
The Pet-sitting Peril
Baby-sitting Is a Dangerous Job
No Monsters in the Closet
Eddie and the Fairy Godpuppy
The Magic Book
Sugar Isn't Everything
Megan's Island
What Could Go Wrong?
Nightmare
To Grandmother's House We Go
Scared Stiff
Jo and the Bandit
What Are We Going to Do About David?
Caught!
The Absolutely True Story . . . How I Visited Yellowstone
   Park with the Terrible Rupes
Twisted Summer
Secrets at Hidden Valley
The Kidnappers

WILLO

DAVIS

ROBERTS

The Kidnappers

a mystery

A JEAN KARL BOOK

ALADDIN PAPERBACKS

For Josh

If you purchased this book without a cover you should be aware that this book is stolen property. It was reported as "unsold and destroyed" to the publisher and neither the author nor the publisher has received any payment for this "stripped book."

First Aladdin Paperbacks edition December 1999

Text copyright © 1998 by Willo Davis Roberts

Aladdin Paperbacks
An imprint of Simon & Schuster Children's Publishing Division
1230 Avenue of the Americas
New York, NY 10020

All rights reserved, including the right of reproduction in whole or in part in any form.
Also available in an Atheneum Books for Young Readers hardcover edition.

Designed by Nina Barnett
The text for this book was set in Goudy.
Printed and bound in the United States of America
10 9 8 7 6 5 4 3

The Library of Congress has cataloged the hardcover edition as follows:
Roberts, Willo Davis.
The kidnappers: a mystery / Willo Davis Roberts.
p.   cm.
"A Jean Karl Book"
Summary: No one believes eleven-year-old Joey, who has a reputation for telling tall tales, when he claims to have witnessed the kidnapping of the class bully outside their expensive private school.
ISBN 0-689-81394-5 (hc.)
[1. Kidnapping—Fiction. 2. Bullies—Fiction.
3. Wealth—Fiction. 4. New York (N.Y.)—Fiction.]
I. Title.
PZ7.R54465Ki   1998
[Fic]—dc21   96-53677
ISBN 0-689-81393-7 (pbk.)

The Kidnappers

a mystery

Chapter One

It's a mistake to earn the reputation of being a liar. It seems harmless enough to make up stories to entertain yourself, but it can backfire. The way it did with me.

On Thursday, Mr. Epperson told us to write a brief personal essay. On the spur of the moment, no time to think about it.

As it happened, I was scared. Too scared to think about anything except meeting Willie after school. So that's what I wrote about.

I was the last one to hand in my paper. Mr. Epperson ran a cursory glance down the page, reading aloud the final sentence. "'He's going to kill me. Dot, dot, dot.' Well, Bishop, if pulp fiction ever makes a comeback, you'll have your niche, all right. In thirty years of teaching I've never had a student who had more imagination than you have."

"I didn't make it up," I said, my voice squeaking a little. "It's true."

He smiled. "Sure it is. See you tomorrow, Bishop."

I don't know how I got through the rest of the afternoon. Everywhere I looked, there was Willie glaring at me. Willie was really William John Edward Groves, III, who stood a head taller than I did and outweighed me by maybe fifteen pounds. Who had taken my elbow in his nose and spouted blood all over the gym during third period, making everyone laugh uproariously.

I'd tried to apologize. I mean, I didn't mean to do it. It was an accident. Not that I'd have cared much, if he hadn't gotten so mad. I didn't especially like Willie.

Willie was picked up from school by limousine, like practically everyone else who attends St. Bart's. I saw him standing just inside the gates, as the rules say we have to do, waiting for his car. He was watching the main front door, but I stayed inside, out of sight. No way was I going to walk out there and let him pound on me. There were even a couple of other kids standing around, probably waiting to see the massacre.

My own car showed up, with Ernie driving. I could see him, waiting in line with other cars, drumming his fingers on the wheel. He wore a uniform cap, and he was distinctive because he always looked as if he needed a shave, even if he'd just had one. He said he'd been that way since he was about fifteen, and he shaved twice a day except on his days off.

Would he rescue me if Willie jumped me on the way to the car? Maybe, but not before Willie got in some good licks. I didn't think he'd be satisfied with anything less than blood—mine—preferably in great quantity in front of as many other kids as possible.

I hesitated, and then I saw that the Groveses' chauffeur had arrived, pulling up and double-parking beyond Ernie. Willie was obviously reluctant to go before I came out, but after the chauffeur leaned out the window and yelled something, Willie gave up and got in the car.

Only after they'd driven away did I emerge, sliding in beside Ernie with a breath of relief.

"What held you up, sport?" Ernie asked, putting the car in gear and easing out into traffic. "You gonna make me late for my date with Alice."

I could tell by the overpowering odor of aftershave that he was going to see Alice. She gave it to him, so I guess she liked it. It made me want to open a window.

"I was waiting for Willie Groves to leave. He was going to kill me."

"Oh, right, well, that's okay, then," Ernie said. He was a big, burly guy, about thirty, I think. He had a thick head of black hair, and he was usually chewing on a toothpick. He said it helped keep him from smoking.

"He said he was going to kill me," I persisted, knowing he didn't believe me. "Because I accidentally gave him a nosebleed in front of everybody else."

Ernie grinned. "Good for you, Joey. Way to go."

"I didn't do it on purpose," I said. "Even if he is a jerk. I don't have any suicide wish."

"How come you riding with me in this traffic, then?" Ernie cut in front of a yellow cab, lifted a finger in response to the honking horn, and eased around the corner in front of a bus.

"I'm close enough to walk home," I said, giving up. "I

don't really need to ride fourteen blocks."

"Oh, you think you're safer out there?" He gestured with a thumb at cars and pedestrians. "Walking these streets, now *there's* a death wish."

I didn't really want to walk home, even if my parents would have allowed it. My brother, Mark, got mugged once and wound up in the emergency room for six stitches in his head.

Ernie slammed on the brakes when a guy stepped off the curb in front of him, and that reminded me to fasten my seat belt before I went through the windshield.

"You and that Willie ain't very good friends, I guess," Ernie said.

"That's an understatement," I muttered. As a matter of fact, I didn't really have very many friends at St. Bart's, except for Pink Murphy. We were the two nerds, the ones who always aced the tests and spoiled everybody else's marks on the curve by coming out higher than the rest of them. My guess was that any guy in school, other than Pink, would have stood around enjoying it if Willie caught me and pounded me silly.

There was no place to pull in at the curb in front of our apartment building, so I got out while Ernie let traffic pile up behind him. Before I got to the front door, Sherman had it open for me. He wore a dark blue uniform, trimmed in gold, and Mother said he gave an air of class to the Upton Towers. Father said he gave it security, which was more to the point.

"Afternoon, Joey," Sherman said. He was a big, bulky man, but fast on his feet, and very strong. Twice I'd seen him pitch someone out of the building, and once I saw him tackle a purse snatcher. "How's it going?"

"Well, I escaped being slaughtered today. Who knows about tomorrow?"

Sherman nodded. "We never know, do we? Your mother's out, your sister's home. Don't know about the rest of the family."

"Okay," I said. "Thanks, Sherman." Sometimes it helped to be forewarned about what I'd be walking into.

If it was only Sophie at home, there was no problem. She was twelve and a half, a year and a half older than I was, and we got along pretty well. It was Mark and my father I had to watch out for.

I took the elevator to the top of the building. I could hear the piano before I unlocked our door. Always, always, Sophie is playing the piano.

Our parents are very proud of my sister's ability on the piano. She's had lessons since she was three, and they have hopes that someday she'll be a renowned concert pianist. Nobody ever has to make her practice; she just loves to play.

I walked into the living room, past the baby grand, pausing until she finished a measure.

"Ho," I said when she stopped.

"Ho," Sophie responded, smiling.

She's the beauty of the family. Dark curls that look better on her than they do on either Mark or me, dark eyes with long lashes. Everybody always knows we're siblings, but nobody ever says Mark and I are good looking, the way they do about Sophie.

"What's to eat?" I asked.

"Fruit or junk? I had a peanut butter and jelly sandwich and some chips."

She followed me into the kitchen and perched on a stool while I made a sandwich and opened a new bag of potato chips.

"I escaped being murdered today," I told her.

"Good. I don't want you to be murdered."

"It may happen tomorrow. Willie carries grudges. He'll be lying in wait for me again."

Her dark eyebrows rose gracefully. "William John Edward Groves, III? What's the matter with him this time?"

I told her.

"Maybe he'll forget it."

"Maybe not." I got a Coke out of the refrigerator and took an adjoining stool. "I wish I could change schools. I hate St. Bart's."

"Mother and Daddy don't want us in public schools," Sophie said.

"It couldn't be any worse, could it? If the kids don't like you, it's no fun."

Sophie is someone other kids like, but she spends so much time playing the piano she doesn't have time to do things with them. It never seems to bother her.

"At least you have good teachers," Sophie pointed out.

"They expect a lot of me."

"That's because you're a genius, Joey. It's why Daddy wants you at St. Bart's. He wants you to live up to your potential."

I snorted. "He wants me to be a banker, like he is. I would hate being a banker."

"When you're grown up, you can be anything you like."

"That's a long time away," I said, taking a swig of Coke. "In the meantime I have to dodge Willie, probably for the rest of my life."

"Why are you dodging Willie?"

We turned toward Mark, who had just come into the kitchen. He's fifteen and thinks he knows everything.

I told the story again.

"And you chickened out and hid?" He was incredulous. "What good did that do you, Joe? He'll still be around tomorrow. Why didn't you just face off with him and give him as good as he gives you?"

"I can't outfight him," I pointed out. "He's taller, heavier, and a better fighter than I am."

"So do the best you can, bloody his nose again if you can, and take whatever he dishes out. At least once he's done it, he shouldn't bother you any further. It would be over and done with."

"And I'd be bloodied and humiliated," I said.

"But if he's going to get you anyway, why prolong the agony? Besides, if you stand up for yourself, people won't be so quick to jump you."

"The only one wanting to jump me is Willie. And I'll lose. Maybe if I stall him for a day or two, he'll give up," I said, knowing that wasn't likely.

"You're such a birdbrain," Mark said in disgust, "but I guess that's appropriate for a chicken, right?"

The evening didn't get any better.

Some nights Father isn't home for dinner, and those are easier. Tonight he was there, and, of course, blabbermouth Mark had to tell him I'd hidden out to keep from having a confrontation with Willie.

Father sighed. He looked at me in the way that makes it clear he is—again—disappointed. "Would you like to take a class in martial arts, Joel?"

"No," I said. I figured I'd really get pulverized in a class of kids learning to kick each other to death.

"Your brother's probably right," Father said after a moment. "The sooner you face this other boy, the sooner you'll put the entire matter behind you."

Easy for him to say, but nobody argued with Father.

"You are growing up. You have to prepare for life as an adult male."

"I intend to write stories. Why do I have to learn to fight to do that?" I demanded.

Father sighed again, more deeply. "Joel, you will have to live in the real world. We've discussed this many times. Writing may be fine as a hobby, but it's unlikely to support you. A good steady job in a bank, working with all kinds of people, is going to be a necessity."

"There are people who earn a living writing," I said, knowing I'd be better off to keep still, because we'd had this discussion before and I'd yet to win any points.

"Not enough of them so you'd notice it," Father said, helping himself to another slice of roast beef. "You don't think it's necessary to earn a steady paycheck, but if you don't have one, you'll soon miss the comforts you have now."

I wanted to yell that I didn't give a darn about the comforts I had now; most of them were things I didn't care about at all, except for the basics of food and shelter. I didn't need to live in a penthouse or be driven around in a Cadillac.

But, of course, nobody yells at my father.

"Writing is a childish dream, Joel," he said.

There are hundreds of publishing companies that must pay something to the thousands of authors whose works they buy. Some books make the best-selling lists, and *those* writers do all right. Why didn't he think it was possible for *me* to do it?

The sensible thing for anyone to do when speaking to my father is to shut up, but I was stubborn.

"I want to write," I said, in a low voice but one that Father could hear.

"Preparing for a lifetime job and writing for the pleasure of it are not mutually exclusive, you know," he said.

Mark put down his fork. "That means you should prepare for the job, and write for a hobby," he explained, as if I didn't understand English.

At this point my mother intervened. "That's enough about this at the table. I dislike mealtimes to be unpleasant. Sophie, we need to decide what you're going to wear to the recital next week. The pale yellow is very pretty, I think."

Sophie groaned. "Mom, it's so babyish! When am I going to have something new, something without ruffles and ribbons?"

I was glad to have the subject turned away from me,

but resentful of how insignificant my problem seemed to everyone else.

After dinner, when Mark had gone to visit a friend down on the sixth floor and everybody else was reading or listening to classical music in the living room, I called Pink from the kitchen phone.

"Does everybody think I'm a coward because I didn't come out and fight Willie this afternoon?" I demanded.

Pink got his name from his complexion and the pinkish gold color of his hair. I could trust him to be honest.

"Well, I didn't hear anybody say anything about that, but a few of them were disappointed. You know, like Willie's buddies, Gene and Paul."

"It just seems silly and pointless to get beat up for nothing," I said helplessly.

"I don't suppose your dad would let you change schools," Pink offered.

"Hah!" I gave a bark of bitter laughter. "Fat chance. Pink, I'm dead meat."

"Maybe not. Maybe something will happen, like he'll break a leg or something before tomorrow."

And maybe it wouldn't, I thought gloomily as I got ready for bed. Maybe by this time tomorrow I'd be dead.

Chapter Two

"Off on another adventure, Joey?" Sherman asked as he held the door for me the following morning.

"Big adventure," I said. "Off to school to be surrounded by enemies. If I don't survive, tell my folks I don't want any flowers at my funeral. They can make a donation to the public library."

"I'll tell 'em," Sherman said solemnly.

Ernie was waiting with the car. "Let's roll, boy. Your dad's got an appointment the other side of town at ten. Don't like to keep the boss waiting."

Everybody referred to Parnell Bishop as my dad. Mark called him Dad, and Sophie called him Daddy, but I never in my life thought of him as anything but Father. As far as I was concerned, he was completely unapproachable. I didn't remember his ever doing anything informal or just for fun. I had never confided in him, and I had no confidence that he would understand if I did. *He* never needed help or advice, and he took it for granted that no one else did, either.

I was prepared to be a nervous wreck all day. Not only Willie but several of his friends kept giving me speaking looks, so I knew what was coming when school got out. It made me sort of sick to my stomach.

Pink stuck as close to me as he could. His round, freckled face had an earnest expression. "You want me to walk out with you tonight?"

I was grateful for the offer, but I turned it down. "It would just get you in trouble, too. Maybe my father's right. I might as well take whatever comes, and hope for the best. At least it'll be over."

During study hall I even managed to fantasize a scene where Willie attacked me and I knocked him flat, right in front of all his buddies.

But when I came out of my last period class, I saw Willie behind me in the hall, and my heart lurched. Mr. Soames, the math teacher, was talking to him, and Willie's back was toward me.

If I got out ahead of him, and Ernie showed up fairly quickly, I could avoid Willie again. There were two days of weekend coming up, that much longer for him to cool down.

I didn't bother to put anything in my locker; I just carried my books and notebook right out the front door and, against the rules, out the gate to the sidewalk.

There were a number of cars lined up, but Ernie wasn't there. Glancing back uneasily, to make sure Willie wasn't coming yet, I decided to move toward the back of the line of cars. Ernie would pick me up there; he'd be sure to spot me before he got in front of the school itself.

St. Bart's is an old school, enclosed inside a high wrought-iron fence. It isn't very big, and it looks especially small compared to the apartment buildings on each side of it.

The apartments go right out to the sidewalk, with no yards. They offered no hiding places, so I started to pray that Ernie wouldn't be late.

I walked toward the corner. Pickup cars eased past me, but there was no Ernie. I hesitated.

Had the Groveses' limo already arrived, and I'd missed it? I glanced back, and saw Willie just emerging from the school.

I didn't think he'd seen me yet. I started to sweat, and then I noticed a delivery truck pulling up, double-parking right in front of me.

The driver jumped out, carrying a good-size carton, heading for the nearest door. He jabbed the bell set into the brick wall, waited a few seconds, and then turned the knob when the lock was released.

I didn't have time to think, and I didn't hesitate. Before the door swung shut behind the deliveryman, I got my foot in front of it and shoved my way inside.

It was just a tiny foyer, with mailboxes on one side and an elevator on the back wall. I watched the indicator rise; the deliveryman had gone up to the fourth floor, and the elevator was staying there for the moment.

There was nowhere for me to go from where I was, not until the elevator came back down.

Through the smudged window in the door I could see the line of cars edging along toward the front of the school, picking up dozens of boys in gray slacks and navy blue sweaters. I'd never especially liked wearing a uniform to school, but it was an advantage in a situation like this. It made it harder to identify any individual. As long as Willie couldn't see my face, he wouldn't know which of all those boys was his target.

How long could I hide in the foyer of the apartment house? What if I'd already missed Ernie when he pulled into the line of cars?

Whether anybody else called me a coward or not, I felt like one. This was a far cry from the heroes in my stories, who always fought and won, or, better yet, outsmarted the enemy with guile and cleverness.

None of the heroes in my imagination ever had been in quite these circumstances, though. I hadn't figured out how this story was supposed to have a happy ending.

The cars slid past in a long line. There was Pink's mom, a nice lady with hair the same color as his, in her station wagon. And Tony Albertoni's mother, in a white Lincoln. And chauffeurs, some in uniform, some not, picking up the string of boys until almost no one was left, except Willie.

Come on, Ernie, I urged silently, but he didn't come.

I heard the elevator behind me and turned around as if I'd just come in, as if I belonged there, to face the deliveryman as he came through the sliding doors.

He didn't pay any attention to me, but went out into the street, dodging between cars to get back into the delivery truck.

And there, just before the door closed to hide me again, was Willie.

I drew a deep breath, but he wasn't looking toward me. He was scowling, his face angry and determined. Through the dirty window I saw that his hands were clenched into fists.

He probably wouldn't hit me more than a couple of times, I thought, trying to slow down my racing heart. And then he'd forget it, he'd be even with me.

The lane of cars beyond him came to an end, and for a moment there were no more in my line of vision. Where the heck was Ernie? Where was Willie's own ride, to take him away from here for a long cooling-off weekend?

How long would Willie stand out there, blocking my escape?

I didn't think he could see me, here in the dimly lighted foyer, but I could see him all right.

And then something even wilder than one of my stories took place.

I saw the emblem as the car crept into view. It was like a family crest or something, in bright colored enamel with gold trim, on a gleaming black door. The car was a Chrysler New Yorker like my grandma Louise's.

The car had very dark windows, so I couldn't make out the driver very well. But just as it came abreast of Willie, the car stopped and the back door opened.

A man jumped out, grabbed Willie from behind, and dragged him into the back of the car. The door slammed, and immediately the Chrysler leaped forward and disappeared from sight.

Afterward I knew I should have jerked open the door and gotten the license number, but I was so stunned I couldn't believe what I'd seen.

Blood thundered in my ears. I could hardly breathe. After a few seconds I threw open the door and stepped out onto the sidewalk.

Half a block away I saw the Chrysler moving rapidly away, too distant for me to identify anything about it.

I might have thought I'd dreamed it except that Willie's books were still lying on the sidewalk, papers spilling out of them. One lined page, with a big red A– written on the top of it, blew into the gutter as I watched.

I swallowed, trying to get more air into my lungs.

Hadn't anybody else seen anything?

There was only one pedestrian, an old man walking with a cane, carrying groceries in a mesh bag. He lifted his head when I spoke to him.

"Did you see it? Did you see them pull him into that car?"

His eyes were blank. He didn't answer, but moved closer to the curb.

"Mister? Somebody just kidnapped that kid!"

The man looked away and scurried on past, leaving me wondering in a panic what to do.

I didn't like Willie Groves, but I didn't hate him enough to want someone to kidnap him.

A horn blared, making me jump. It was only a driver objecting to somebody cutting him off, and I saw to my relief that it was Ernie, at last.

I ran around the front of the car and fell into the seat

beside him. "Ernie, we've got to call the police! Willie was just kidnapped!"

He put the car in gear and eased into traffic. "Well, that settles the little problem you had yesterday, don't it?"

"No, seriously, Ernie, it really happened! This big black Chrysler pulled up beside Willie, and a guy jumped out and hauled him into the backseat, and they drove away before I could get the license number!"

"The cops ain't gonna like it that you didn't get the number," Ernie said, making the corner to head for home. "What kind of a detective are you going to make, Joey?"

I jerked desperately on his arm. "I'm not kidding, honest! He's really been kidnapped!"

"Couldn't of happened to a nicer kid, right? Listen, your mom asked me to stop and pick up some stuff for tomorrow's party, okay? Sit tight while I run in and get it."

I stared at him incredulously. He wasn't taking me seriously at all. "Give me the phone," I said.

The cellular bag was usually right there beside him on the seat, but it wasn't there now. "Where is it?" I demanded.

"The phone? Had a slight mishap with it," Eddie said. "Dropped it and somebody ran over it before I could retrieve it. Gonna have to get a new one. What do you need a phone for? You'll be home in a few minutes."

"I need to call the police."

"You better reconsider that, maybe," Ernie advised. "The cops don't like practical jokes. Friend of mine made a call reporting a nonexistent crime, once, and they threw him in the clink. Missed his own birthday party. The rest of us had fun, though."

He swung the car into a left turn, double-parked outside the place where my mom got her party decorations, and bailed out with the motor running to dash inside.

There wasn't a pay phone in sight. I wondered wildly if I could run home faster than I'd get there by waiting for Ernie, but I didn't think so. He was back in a few minutes with an armload of boxes, which he threw in the trunk, then went back for more before he finally slid into the driver's seat again.

"Listen," I said desperately, "this isn't a story, it's *real*. We've got to tell the police!"

"Bad thinking, Joey. Listen, I'm having a bad day. Got into a fender bender and got to school late, and then I had to get this stuff for your mom, and I just don't have what it takes to listen to dinosaurs on the roof or a fire in the Dumpster, okay?"

"There *was* a fire in the Dumpster," I said, half angrily, "and I was only six when I told about the dinosaurs. I didn't make this up, I swear!"

"If you'll carry half this stuff, I won't have to make two trips," Ernie said, then yelled out the open window, "Watch it, buddy, I'm already using this lane!"

It was no use. He wasn't going to take me seriously. Why hadn't I picked up Willie's books? Just because Ernie came then and I was scared? The books would have proved something, wouldn't they? Would anybody find them? Would Willie get in trouble if they were lost?

What was I thinking? Willie was *already* in worse

trouble than losing a few books and papers. He'd been kidnapped! I should have left Ernie sitting in the car and run back into the school to report it.

And then I remembered Mr. Sciotti's reaction to my hoax about the rat in the bathroom the day school started, and decided maybe it would be safer to leave the school out of it.

As soon as we pulled up in front of the Upton Towers, I bolted out of the car, but Ernie caught me by the back of the neck before I got very far.

"Slow down, cowboy. You're helping me with this stuff, remember? You take the two little boxes, and I'll get the rest of it."

"Ernie, please, this isn't one of my tall stories, I promise! I really do have to call the cops!"

"Well, it's your hide, not mine. You can call them as soon as we get this stuff upstairs. Thank you, Sherman. Nice day, isn't it?"

"Indeed. Beautiful October." Sherman was smiling, but I couldn't smile back. I didn't think it was worth telling him my story, but Ernie had paused when Sherman held the door open.

"Joey's in fine form today. Witnessed a kidnapping of the kid who was going to kill him this afternoon."

"Well, well." Sherman was beaming. "That's a good solution, isn't it? Mrs. Bishop just called down to see if you had arrived yet, said you were running late."

"Had a fender bender. Some cretin scratched my right front. Mr. Bishop's not going to be very happy with me, but the guy who caused it had more damage than I did.

Don't know why I want to make a living driving in this town."

I wanted to smash them both. Why couldn't they see that this time I wasn't playing jokes? I stormed on past Sherman, stepped into the waiting elevator, and punched the button. I didn't care if Ernie made it on this trip or not.

He got a foot into the opening before the doors closed. "You mad at me, Joey?" he asked, getting a better grip on the boxes he carried.

"You won't listen to me," I said. "It's real. It's serious."

This time he didn't crack a grin. "Okay. I'll listen on the way up. Somebody snatched this little punk . . . where? Right in front of the school with everybody watching? And nobody else noticed?"

"Everybody else was already gone." I still didn't think he was giving me the benefit of the doubt, but I felt compelled to tell him anyway. "I had ducked into the foyer of that apartment house right next to the school, and I could see out the window. Willie was looking around to see where I'd gone, and this car drove up real slow—a black Chrysler with a fancy emblem on the door, like royalty—and a guy jumped out and dragged Willie into the backseat.

"You see the driver? What did he look like?" Ernie sounded half convinced.

"The windows were black glass. I couldn't see through them. But," I added in a spurt of words I hadn't known I was going to say until they came out, "I *did* get a look at the guy who grabbed him."

"Yeah?" We stopped at the sixth floor, and a woman

carrying a briefcase got on. "We're going up, ma'am."

"So am I. Eighth floor," she said pleasantly, and we didn't say any more until she got off a few moments later. Then Ernie asked, "What did he look like?"

It was funny. I could see the face really plain, but there wasn't anything particularly distinctive about it. "I don't know. Youngish. Older than Mark, but younger than you. Twenty-four, twenty-five, maybe?"

"Dark? Blond? Identifying tattoos?"

I screwed up my face, trying to remember. "Dark. Yeah, dark hair, like mine and yours. Just an ordinary face. No scars or tattoos."

"Makes a better story if he had a unique tattoo. Like, a serpent running up his arm, or a shapely lady on his biceps."

He didn't believe me after all, I thought angrily. He was starting to smile again.

"Build? The cops always want to know the perp's build. Big? Little? Fat? Skinny?"

I had to think again. "He moved fast, and I never saw him standing up straight. Average height, I guess. Not big, but he had muscles. He was wearing a white T-shirt, and he had strong arms."

"Well, they ought to be able to narrow it down from that description," Ernie said, stepping forward as the elevator doors slid open. "Can't apply to more than half the men in the city. Get that door, will you?"

Anxious and frustrated, I followed him into our apartment, wondering if I'd have any better luck with the police than I was having with Ernie.

A part of me was sort of glad Willie was getting what he deserved instead of pounding on me. But I was uneasy, speculating on what was going to happen to Willie if I didn't report the kidnapping to the cops right away. I didn't think I hated him enough to want to see on the six o'clock news that somebody'd found his body in an alley.

The sooner I reported this the better.

Chapter Three

Usually our apartment is like a tomb except for the music. If Mom or Sophie is home, there is classical music, either on the piano or on CDs. If Mark is home by himself, there is rock or jazz or rap. If there is only me, I prefer books and silence. Father objects to Mark's music if it penetrates as far as the room where he's working or reading. He never comments on anything else.

That day we were assaulted by noise the minute we walked in.

It was Junie's day to clean, and she was running the vacuum cleaner. Sophie was practicing, something loud and fast that I'd never heard before. Ernie came as far in as the dining room, where he unloaded his packages alongside the ones that were already there.

He gave me a pat on the shoulder. "Keep up the good work, Joey. You'll banish all the demons and dragons yet."

I didn't answer him. The heck with him. He'd be talking out the other side of his mouth when he read in the paper that Willie had been rescued from the foulest of kidnappers because of evidence provided by Joel Bishop, age eleven.

It was impossible to talk on the living room phone because of Junie's vacuum cleaner. I dumped my own load of packages and headed for the kitchen.

The dishwasher was running, and my mother was standing at the phone, covering one ear with a hand to screen out the worst of the racket.

"But Mr. DeForest promised them to me by tomorrow morning!" she exclaimed as I walked in. "The party is tomorrow evening at eight, and it will take at least an hour to arrange them all. I can't be doing flowers at the last split second. There are too many other last-minute things to do."

She glanced around, acknowledging me with a nod.

Silently, I mouthed the words, *I need to use the phone.*

She shook her head and mouthed back, *Not now.*

Mark had his own phone. I headed for his bedroom.

Unfortunately, he was there. Sprawled on the bed with the phone screwed into his ear.

He stared at me with annoyance.

"Can I use your phone?" I asked. "I need to call the police."

His eyebrows went up. "I'll call you back, Tracy," he said into the receiver, and then hung up. But he didn't hand the phone to me.

"What in heck for?"

I swallowed and willed him to believe me. "I saw a kidnapping take place. I need to report it."

My brother groaned. "Not now, Joe. I'm having an

important conversation, and I don't have time for this. I thought you were serious."

"I *am* serious. I saw a kidnapping, Mark."

"Who got kidnapped?" He didn't bother to conceal his skepticism.

"Willie Groves. This black New Yorker stopped, and a guy got out and grabbed Willie and threw him in the car, and they roared away before I could get the license number, and—"

Mark scowled. "Joey, you're so full of crap I wouldn't believe you if you said the house was on fire and I could smell the smoke. Get out of here." He started dialing and turned his back on me.

For a few seconds I considered jumping on top of him and wrestling the phone away from him. Better judgment changed my mind. He's even bigger than Willie, and the last time I had wrestled with him he sprained my wrist and we knocked over a lamp and were both grounded for a week.

There was yet a third telephone line in the place, but I'd never used it. It was in Father's study, and nobody was supposed to touch it but him.

There was no reason to think Father would be home for another couple of hours.

This was urgent. The cops were probably going to be mad that it had taken me this long to make a report.

I walked past Mom, still arguing with someone on the kitchen phone. Past Sophie thundering on the piano. Past Junie in her white ankle socks and athletic shoes with her black uniform encasing her like an overstuffed sausage.

She gave me a smile but didn't try to talk over the

racket. For once I couldn't smile back.

The minute I walked into the study I felt like a trespasser. Well, I *was*. The only times I'd ever been in it before had been when I was delivering something or getting dressed down for something.

I closed the door behind me and crossed the deep green carpet to the impressive desk. There was nothing on it except the phone, a pen and pencil set, and a notepad with nothing written on it.

Now that I was ready to call, I was almost paralyzed. My fingers were cold as I dialed 9-1-1.

I was so panicky that I didn't even hear the words spoken by the calm voice, but I knew it had to be the emergency operator.

"I . . . I need to talk to someone about a kidnapping," I said, thankful that I didn't squeak.

"A kidnapping? Your name, please."

"Uh . . . Joe Bishop," I said, sounding as if I wasn't sure about it. "There's this kid from my school. I saw a car stop and drag him inside. I didn't get the license number, but it was a black Chrysler New Yorker, this year's model, I'm pretty sure."

There was a small silence before the man's voice came back on, brisk and cool. "Look, son. This is an emergency line. We have no time for practical jokers. In fact, it's a crime to make false reports. You could wind up before a judge for this kind of thing."

"No, wait! This isn't a joke, it really happened! You've got to listen to me! The kid's name is Willie Groves, his dad's the head of—"

The man had hung up. I stared in disbelief at the phone. The police were supposed to help you, not write you off as some kind of kook.

The door opened and my mother stood there looking at me. And not as if she were pleased with me. "What are you doing in here, Joel?"

"Using the phone. I was trying to call the police, but the guy wouldn't listen to me—"

"The police? What for?"

"Mom, nobody believes me, but it's true, I swear it! I was sort of hiding from Willie Groves. He was chasing me. There was this car that drove up beside him and a guy pulled Willie into the backseat and they drove away! Willie dropped his books on the sidewalk, and they kidnapped him! Honest!"

She stared at me for another few seconds, then sighed. "Joey, don't get into another one of your dramatic presentations. We have a major event planned for tomorrow evening, and there are still dozens of things to see to. I don't have time for this. And you know you're not supposed to be in your father's study. He hates to have anyone touch his things."

I got up from Father's chair, feeling like screaming. How could I get someone to listen to me?

"Call Willie's folks, then! They'll tell you he didn't come home from school! They'll tell you he's missing!"

For a few seconds I thought she was halfway convinced that I was on the level. Then she turned away. "Come out of here before anyone else sees you. Your father would be most unhappy if he knew you'd been in here."

"Please, Mom! It would only take a minute to call and find out for sure!"

She wavered, and I pulled open drawers, looking for the phone book. "I'll find it, the number. Call them!"

So she did. My heart was tearing my chest apart, making a thundering in my ears where the blood was racing out of control.

"Hello, Mrs. Groves? Oh, this is Joel Bishop's mother. Is Mrs. Groves available?"

I held my breath.

"I see. Well, can you tell me if Willie is home from school yet?"

Whoever was on the other end of the line said something, and my mother's expression changed. There was no belief there now as she fixed her gaze on me. "I see. Thank you." She dropped the phone into its cradle. "Mrs. Groves has gone to Boston for a few days because of her mother's illness. And Willie isn't home because the chauffeur called half an hour ago to say he'd been delayed because of a minor accident. But the maid didn't think there was anything wrong at all."

"But the chauffeur didn't pick him up! He hadn't come by the time somebody kidnapped Willie."

She walked across the room, herding me ahead of her into the hallway. "Did you tell this story to anyone at St. Bart's?"

"No. Ernie came, and I told him, but he didn't believe me and wouldn't let me stop to telephone the police—"

"I shouldn't wonder. Joey, an imagination is a wonderful thing, very entertaining, but there are limits.

Nothing truly catastrophic has happened because of your tall stories, so far, but this one might result in our having to get a lawyer to keep you out of juvenile hall! Do you realize that? Have you thought what your father's reaction would be if the police actually came here to question you?"

I was thinking of it now. I remember he turned purple the time I set the trap to get even with Mark—after he'd destroyed some of my history papers so I had to redo them—and Father was the one who got drenched with the bucket of water when he went into Mark's room. And *that* had been relatively harmless.

For a moment I wondered wildly if maybe I *had* imagined the whole thing. Had I had so much practice trying to put things over on other people for the fun of it (mine) that I'd finally slipped over the edge and was believing one of my own stories?

But no.

I had seen Willie. I had seen the black New Yorker with the royal-looking emblem. I had seen a muscular dark-haired man grab Willie from behind and drag him into the car against his will. But everyone thought I was lying.

So what did I do now?

Chapter Four

"Sooner or later," Sophie said, "his family will know he's been kidnapped, Joey. They probably know by now."

It was after dinner. We were sitting cross-legged on her frilly pink and white bedspread in her ruffled pink and white bedroom, decorated the way Mom thought was appropriate for a preteen.

"How are we going to find out?" I asked earnestly. "I'm going crazy wondering if they've killed him by this time."

"Why would they kill Willie? Kidnapping is usually for ransom, isn't it? So they'd probably send a note demanding money," Sophie pointed out. "Or they could take him as a threat to his father—to blackmail him into doing what they want, or something like that. But most likely it's for ransom."

"So what do I do now?" I demanded. "Nobody will listen to me! Only you, and Pink, when I call him."

Sophie hesitated. "We could call again and see if Willie ever came home from school. It's been a long time since Mom tried."

I knew Willie hadn't gone home, but I didn't know what else to do. We had to look the number up again, at the kitchen phone. Sophie was less upset than I was, so she was the one who asked for Willie.

It was obviously a maid who answered. They must have someone who lived in, not a twice-a-week cleaning woman like Junie. Willie was not available to answer the phone, Sophie was told. So she asked for Mr. Groves.

She listened a moment, then replaced the receiver. Her eyes were very big. "She said Mr. Groves isn't taking any calls."

"So what does that mean? Is Willie missing and they're dealing with the kidnappers? Have they already reported to the police?"

"Maybe," Sophie said. "By this time they have to know there's something wrong if Willie's not there."

We didn't know what else to do. On TV the family of someone who's been kidnapped negotiates directly with the kidnappers, without going to the police for fear the person who's been kidnapped will be harmed. Other times the police are in the home monitoring the phone, directing the delivery of ransom money in hopes of catching the criminals.

There was no way the cops would tell me anything even if they knew what was going on. But they didn't know what I had seen.

I was practically shaking, but there was only one thing I could think of to try. "The police would listen to an adult. I'm going to have to tell Father and hope he'll call them for me."

That turned out to be a total bust, too.

My father was working in his study. He was irritated because my mother kept asking for his opinion on things to do with the party, and he was definitely unhappy when I showed up.

Sophie had gone with me, but he ignored her and glared at me.

"Joel, how many times have I asked you not to bother me when I'm busy? I have to fax these papers off yet tonight, and I don't have time to talk to you."

Sophie spoke while I was still working my throat, trying to make some convincing words come out.

"It's important, Daddy. Joey saw something important, and the police need to know about it. But because he's a kid, they think he's playing practical jokes or something. Please listen to him."

"The police?" Father's voice was sharp. "What have you gotten mixed up in this time? When are you going to grow up enough to stop all this foolishness? You can't expect me to go on forever talking you out of trouble. If this is school business, talk to Mr. Giacomo. I've already told him you're old enough to take responsibility for your own actions."

"It's not about school," I said desperately, ashamed that my voice had a tremor in it. "Not directly, anyway. I was . . . trying to keep out of Willie Groves's way, and he followed me. But he hadn't found me, and a car came up and somebody grabbed him and pulled him into the backseat. I didn't see the license number, but I did see the car, and maybe that would help the police to find him. He dropped his books and stuff on the sidewalk. Maybe somebody found them. And his folks must know he's missing by this time, only the maid says Mr. Groves isn't taking any calls—"

Father made a rude sound. "I shouldn't wonder he doesn't want to talk to smart-alecky kids."

"But if Willie's been kidnapped, he surely wants to know about any clues that were left behind, doesn't he? And I was the only one who saw it happen!" I was pleading with him to believe me. "Maybe he'd talk to you, and you could tell him about the black New Yorker with the fancy emblem on the door. That's not the greatest clue, not without a license number, but it's something, isn't it? It might help?"

I braced for his refusal to get involved. For another lecture.

"If this is another one of your pranks, Joel—"

"It's not! It really happened!" I said quickly.

At the same time Sophie chimed in, "Please try, Daddy. Joey's not making it up this time—"

His gaze rested on my sister. "Did you see it? This kidnapping?"

"No," she had to admit. "But I know he's telling the truth. Please, Daddy. See if you can get Mr. Groves to talk to you. Even if he won't admit Willie's gone, if you tell him about the car and the man—"

For the first time he eyed me without total rejection of what I was saying. "You could identify the man who took him?"

"Yes, I think so. If I saw him again."

He hesitated for only a few seconds. "What's the Groveses' number?"

Relief swept over me in a wave that made me almost sick.

But the relief was premature. Father, too, was told that Mr. Groves was not taking any phone calls this evening. "All right," he said into the receiver. "When he's available, please have him call Parnell Bishop." He recited his phone number. "And tell him it's urgent, if you would. Tell him it has to do with his son, Willie."

I slumped into a chair. "So we're right back where we started."

"Not quite," Father said. For him, he sounded reasonable. "I've left a message, and eventually he'll return the call. If Willie *is* missing, Mr. Groves is undoubtedly very busy and very worried."

"Shouldn't we call the police, then?" Sophie asked, twisting her hands together.

Father considered. It was one of the few times I could recall that he hadn't made an instantaneous decision. "No. I think not. If there *was* a kidnapping and he's not yet called in the police, for whatever reason, I don't want to cause further complications. A kidnapper might have threatened to harm Willie unless a ransom is paid without notifying the authorities. That's not a decision I would like to make, if it were one of my children."

"Wouldn't you call the police?" I demanded, surprised to be talking to him this way.

"I think now that I would. But each case is different, and I can't know the circumstances in this one. Perhaps not. Perhaps if your lives were at risk, or Mark's, I would have to reconsider."

"So we can't do any more?" I asked in despair.

"Not for the moment. If I haven't heard from Bill Groves by tomorrow morning, I'll try again to reach him. And this had darned well better be on the level, Joel. Otherwise, you'll find yourself grounded for the rest of your life. Understand?"

"I'm telling the truth," I muttered.

"Now let me finish this paperwork," Father said. So we left his study.

Sophie went back to practicing on the piano, and Mom was watching some soapy movie in the living room. I tried to watch TV in my room. I couldn't get into a program, though. I flipped all around the channels and nothing caught my attention.

Where was Willie? Who had taken him, and why? For money? How long would it be before a ransom could be paid, *if* it could be? What if it was a million dollars? Could Mr. Groves come up with that much? Was Willie hurt? Was he scared?

He had to be scared. I could imagine myself in such a predicament, and I'd be terrified. I remembered a true story I heard about what had happened a long time ago, where kidnappers or terrorists had taken the grandson of a famous millionaire. To prove they had him, and to coerce the payment to them of a tremendous amount of money, they had cut off the boy's ear and sent it to the grandfather through the mail.

I imagined opening up the box and seeing that ear.

For a few seconds I thought I was going to throw up.

Usually I could entertain myself by making up stories. Some of them had me as the starring player, and I would have great adventures, perform incredible rescues, be the hero I'd probably never be in real life. I could lose myself in fantasy.

Tonight it didn't work.

My imagination was still working, all right. But it wasn't a distraction, it drove me crazy.

I pictured Willie in a cellar, lying on gunnysacks in a coal bin, his hands tied behind him, a strip of duct tape across his mouth so he couldn't scream.

I saw Willie in the back of a car, on the floor with a blanket over him so nobody could tell he was a captive, choking on a gag they'd put in his mouth.

I pictured him tied to a chair while somebody tortured him, trying to make him talk. I couldn't think what Willie would know that anyone would try to force out of him, but the image wouldn't go away.

I'd made up stories about people before. I'd enjoyed thinking about my brother lying mangled in the middle of the street, after he'd tattled on me for having tried one of our grandpa's cigars. Father grounded me for a week. Once I imagined staking Father out on a bed of fire ants for being so unfair when Mark started a fight and he blamed me. It wasn't even me who broke the lamp, but I ended up paying for it.

I'd had thoughts about Willie before, too. I'd have been too chicken to bloody his nose on purpose, but I would have taken a lot of satisfaction in seeing it happen if I hadn't known he'd retaliate.

If I knew for sure that Willie would be rescued, I wouldn't care if he suffered a little bit. But I didn't want it on my conscience that bad things happened to him because I didn't do what my grandma would call my Christian duty in reporting the kidnapping.

I fell asleep with the light on. Once I woke up when a telephone rang, but I knew at once it was the one in Mark's room, not in Father's study. I heard him answer it, then laugh. I wondered how long it would take me to feel amused again, if they didn't rescue Willie before it was too late.

I almost forgot that I'd been hiding from Willie because he wanted to beat me up. I almost forgot what a jerk he usually was. I couldn't forget that this time it wasn't one of my stories, his predicament was real.

I reached out and turned off the light before I fell asleep again.

And in my dreams the saga continued. Willie, bloody nose spouting all over his hand. Willie, spluttering through the wad of paper towels the coach had handed him. Willie, cussing me out once the coach walked away. Threatening me. Lying in wait for me in front of the school.

It was as real as when it actually happened. And then I saw his bewildered face when he was looking for me. And the black car with the classy emblem, and the back door being thrown open, and the man getting an arm around Willie's neck from behind, then dragging him into the car.

A youngish man, with dark hair, and an ordinary white T-shirt, and there was the glint of a gold watch on one wrist, and a matching glimmer, hardly more than a speck, of gold in one ear.

An earring. A tiny thin gold hoop.

The kidnapper had worn a watch and an earring.

I came wide awake, remembering.

Did I really see the watch and the earring? Or had I only dreamed it?

I was sweating and gasping for breath.

I lay there in the dark, trying not for the dream, but for the reality of what I'd seen from behind that smudged glass of the apartment house foyer.

I'd remembered two more clues: a gold watch and an earring.

Not much, maybe, when so many men wore watches and earrings.

I wanted to tell my father, so when Mr. Groves called back he would get all the clues that might save Willie.

Only when I got up and crept through the darkened apartment to stand outside my parents' bedroom door, there was no sound or light behind it. My father was asleep.

After I stood there for a few seconds, I even heard his soft snoring.

I hesitated. There was a strong urge to knock and wake him up, to tell him what I'd remembered.

And then I remembered even more clearly how he'd reacted to previous things I'd related, before I learned that there were better people to try them on than Father.

Some of them had been tall tales, but some of them had been true, like the time I saw a guy get bitten by a dog and have to be taken away in an ambulance, or the time a street person built a fire in the Dumpster in the alley.

I was reminded of the fact that this was one of the few times that my father had even partially believed me. If what I'd said didn't pan out when he finally talked to Willie's dad, I was dead meat.

After a minute or so I turned and went back to my own room. I'd tell him first thing in the morning.

Chapter Five

I woke up feeling uneasy without knowing why. Only when I came fully awake did it come back to me.

I bounded out of bed. In daylight, now, I was sure I had really seen the watch and the earring. Without even bothering to get dressed, I dashed out of my room.

And dashed right back into it and slammed the door. The place was full of strangers.

I stood for a moment, digesting what I'd seen. Men carrying things I hadn't recognized. Women carrying flowers. Some guy lugging a cello case.

The party! Of course, tonight my parents were having a big important party for a lot of big shots, important people. Bankers and college presidents and I thought maybe some musicians and an actor or two.

There would be live music, but the musicians wouldn't be here at this time of the day. I checked the clock to make sure it was only eight-thirty in the morning, that I hadn't somehow slept all day.

I scrabbled around for clothes and got dressed.

Mark ran into me in the hallway.

"If I were you, I'd plan to be somewhere else until this is over," he advised. "It's a madhouse, and if you even look at Mom she comes unglued."

"Where are you going?" I asked uncertainly.

"Anywhere out of here. Downstairs to Andy's. Out to somewhere private."

He was gone, melding in with people doing incomprehensible things in the living room, the dining room. Mom was in the kitchen, on the phone again. She didn't pay any attention to me, and I opened the refrigerator to find something to eat.

I had just opened a bottle of orange juice when she stopped me. "Joel, don't touch that, it's for the party. Leave all the juices. And don't get in anybody's way."

"Am I allowed to eat something? Or do I get spending money to go out? I need to talk to Father. Has he had breakfast yet?"

"He left half an hour ago. Something urgent. He had a telephone call. I don't know why they have to bother him on Saturdays."

"A call from Mr. Groves?" I asked, forgetting about food.

"No, I don't think so. Just his office."

"So who'll take his call, then? Father left a message for him to call back as soon as possible. And I've remembered something that might be important."

"Well, your dad's not here. Please, Joel, cooperate for once in your life, will you? Stay out from under foot."

"If I can't eat here, can I have some money to go to Moroney's or somewhere?"

"My purse is on my dressing table. Take what you need," she said, and turned back to the phone.

"Can I get in on that, too?" It was Mark, not yet gone, and he followed me along to our parents' room. Junie was there, putting things to rights.

"Hey, how come you're working today?" I asked, spotting the purse and heading for it.

"The party, stupid," Mark said without rancor. "I'm surprised Mom hasn't got *us* down on our hands and knees scrubbing bathrooms with toothbrushes."

"I did that yesterday," Junie said. She's about as old as Grandma Louise, and her knees hurt, but she has to work because Social Security isn't enough to live on. "Time and a half today, plus a bonus if everything comes off all right. Which it will, if you guys take a hike."

"Thanks for the vote of confidence in us, Junie," Mark said, taking the purse out of my hands and opening it up. "Enough for breakfast, lunch, and maybe for a movie this afternoon. When do you think it will be safe to come home?"

Junie made a face. "Tomorrow morning?"

"Aren't we going to get dinner, even?" I asked, appalled.

"I think your mother is intending you should heat up a TV dinner in the microwave," Junie said. "Eat it in your room, so you don't mess anything up."

"Terrific. I suppose we aren't supposed to emerge from isolation during the party, either." Mark handed the purse to me. "Get enough to last all day, Joe. Otherwise you might starve before we're allowed back in the kitchen."

With that advice he vanished, stuffing some bills into his wallet.

I hesitated, then took enough money to pay Pink's way, too, in case he wanted to keep me company. I decided to call him from the phone in here, if Mom wasn't still tying up the line.

She wasn't. Pink wasn't up yet, his mom said, but she'd call him.

While I waited I thought about Willie. It seemed as if his dad would have called back by now, after Father said it was urgent. I asked Junie if she'd taken any calls.

She rolled her eyes. "Took one call that sent Mr. Bishop off like there was a firecracker stuck in his pocket. Three or four calls Mrs. Bishop answered. And then another one for your father, but by that time he wasn't here."

"Do you know who it was? He was expecting a call from Willie's dad, Mr. Groves."

"I guess that's who it was. I had to say I didn't know when Mr. Bishop would be back."

I stared at her in dismay. "But we were going to tell him I saw Willie get kidnapped! So he could tell the police about the car and what one of the kidnappers looked like!"

"Bad thing to get mixed up in, a kidnapping," Junie said, as if I'd been talking about somebody losing a glove or something equally unimportant. "I hope you never get in bad trouble again, Joey, for making up all this stuff. I don't know where your imagination comes from. Certainly your parents don't have any."

"This isn't my—oh, hi, Pink. I've got breakfast money. Want to meet me at the deli? I guess we've been kicked out of the house today because of the party tonight. Mark took enough to go to a movie, too."

"Okay," Pink agreed at once. "Shall I meet you at Moroney's?"

"Yeah. Twenty minutes?"

"Make it half an hour. I'm not dressed yet. Okay?"

I agreed and was about to try again to make Junie understand that I was serious, when Sophie showed up in the doorway.

"Do you have to get out, too?" I asked her.

"No. I can practice until the musicians arrive. It's a string sextet. Allowing enough time to set up chairs before they start. I think they're going to be served a buffet supper about seven. Did Daddy talk to Mr. Groves?"

"No," I told her bitterly, and explained.

Only then did I notice she was carrying the morning paper. "I looked in the *Herald* and there's nothing about a kidnapping. Maybe you misunderstood what you saw, Joey."

"Oh, sure. How many explanations are there for a kid getting jerked into the back of a car, spilling his stuff all over the sidewalk, and being carried away? You looked through the whole paper?"

"Well, the parts where I thought a kidnapping would be reported. What are you going to do now?"

"What can I do, until Father comes home? Listen, if Mr. Groves calls back, would *you* try to explain? Tell him Father will verify my story?"

Sophie looked doubtful. "Well, as crazy as this place is

today, it would be a miracle if I intercepted the phone call. But I'll try."

A lady with a cart loaded with flowers got off the elevator when I went out in the hall. How many more flowers did we need, for pete's sake?

Ernie got off the elevator, too.

He greeted me with a grin. "How's it going, Joey?"

"Rotten. Nobody believes anything I say."

The elevator doors started to slide closed behind him, and I caught and held them.

"Well, when you've spent your entire life trying to con people into believing things like there's a spaceship on the roof, what do you expect? You ever read the story about the boy who cried 'wolf'?"

"There *was* a spaceship on the roof, and it looked real from where I was standing. How did I know some guys built it out of paper or something, for a party."

"Yep." Ernie was amiable, as usual. "So, you off the kidnapping kick today, are you?"

"No. That was real, even if nobody thinks so. Well, maybe my father believes me, a little bit."

"He does?" Ernie looked at me sharply. "How'd you manage that?"

"I just told him. Had him call Willie's dad, to see if Willie was missing."

"And was he?"

"We didn't find out. Nobody would take Father's call, and then when Mr. Groves *did* call back, Father was already gone. There was nothing in the paper this morning. Sophie looked."

Ernie nodded. "I gotta run. Your mom has some errands for me. I never saw a party that was this much work to set up, but at least I'm getting overtime today. Alice has been wanting to see that new musical, so maybe this'll pay for it. See you later, kid."

"Ernie, I *did* see what happened to Willie. And I remembered something I didn't remember yesterday."

"Oh? What's that? Get that license number after all?"

"No. But I remembered something about the guy who pulled Willie into the car. He was wearing a gold watch, looked like an expensive one, and a tiny gold earring."

Ernie looked impressed. "That might help, if you can get anybody to listen. A tattoo, though, that would make for a more positive identification. Sure you wouldn't rather try a tattoo?"

Laughing, he headed for our front door.

I got in the elevator and punched the button for the lobby. At least Sophie and Pink believed me.

Moroney's Deli is on the corner. I got there ahead of Pink and looked over the cases. You can get anything, any time of day, at Moroney's. All kinds of salads, antipasto, sandwiches, giant dill pickles, cheese cake, Greek pastries, meatballs and spaghetti.

It smelled great. I had mine all picked out by the time Pink got there, and he'd been thinking about it, so it didn't take long to get it all together.

Moroney's only has three tables, and they were full. We didn't want to eat there, anyway. Instead, we took our brown paper bags and headed along the street to the edge of the park.

There were some guys shooting baskets there and a few little kids on the swings and the slide. We found a bench in the sun, which felt good, and ate breakfast. Hot pastrami for me, lasagne and pickles for Pink. He always has pickles, no matter what else he eats. We finished off with a bag of potato chips.

"You got enough cash for lunch, too?" Pink asked as he licked his fingers.

"Yeah. The way it sounds, I should have taken money for supper, too. I don't think I'm going to be allowed in the kitchen. I ought to go back home, though, and see if Willie's dad's called yet."

"Call," Pink suggested, indicating a pay phone on the corner. So I did, and got Junie, who said there had been a gazillion calls, but none of them was Mr. Groves, and no, Father hadn't come back yet.

"It's driving me nuts, Pink," I told him as we walked along the edge of the park. "What if they've done something terrible to Willie? What if they've even killed him?"

"Not much profit in that," Pink pointed out. "It'd make more sense if they collected ransom. Why don't we go over there and see if we can poke around and find out anything?"

"Go over where? To his house?"

"It's an apartment building only about a mile from St. Bart's. I was there once. His mom planned a surprise birthday party for him when he was eight. Great party. He wasn't such a jerk in those days."

Neither of us was supposed to be wandering around without telling anyone where we were going, but both our mothers thought we were at Moroney's and just hanging around the park. We could walk to Willie's, and on a bright Saturday morning it didn't seem very dangerous.

So we walked, and talked until we arrived.

The Groveses lived on the eighth floor of his building, but we couldn't get up there.

The doorman was a snooty guy in uniform, not at all friendly or helpful. Finally, we gave up and went back onto the street.

It was getting warmer, now, and more people were out walking their dogs, running errands. Traffic was heavier, too.

"Let's walk home past St. Bart's," I said finally. "See if there are any clues left where they grabbed him. See if anybody picked up his stuff. Maybe if I had something with his name on it, somebody would listen."

We were halfway across the street when a yellow cab came out of nowhere, roaring straight at us.

Chapter Six

The only reason it didn't kill us was that a parked red Camaro had started to pull out just before the cab sped around the corner. There was a squeal of brakes, and the cab dodged the car, clipping its left front fender with a shriek of metal before it tore away.

Pink and I had taken a dive toward the curb, falling between a parked car and the red Camaro. We were lucky not to get squashed between the Camaro and the car behind it when the Camaro was hit.

Even without being struck by one of the cars, we got banged up. I hit my head on something and scraped my hands. Pink pulled up his pants leg to look at his knee while I sat up and looked around.

"Scraped the skin off," he pronounced, "but it's not bad. Man, that guy was a maniac!"

The driver of the red Camaro was out of his car, staring after the retreating cab, swearing a blue streak. "Hit and run! He banged up my car and he never even stopped!"

"Are you boys hurt?" an elderly lady asked, pausing beside us. "The drivers are so terrible these days."

A few people stopped, though most of them didn't bother. It takes real blood to draw people to a wreck, not skinned knees and a dented fender. One observer asked, "Did anybody get a license number?" But nobody had. It was all over too quickly.

Nobody called the police. There was no way to trace the culprit; there were more yellow cabs than private cars on the streets.

"It was an old one, beat up," Pink said.

That didn't distinguish it much, I thought, rubbing the grit out of my hand. The knee I'd landed on was beginning to smart, too, but I didn't bother to look at it. "You okay, Pink?"

"I guess so." He straightened up and sucked in a deep breath. "Boy, I thought we were goners."

"Yeah. I guess we can walk, though, huh?"

Before we'd gone very far I realized I'd bruised a hip, maybe on the back bumper of the Camaro, and Pink thought he'd twisted his back. We kind of limped along, and since we'd already crossed the street we kept going toward St. Bart's.

"Boy," I said after we'd walked a few blocks, "I'll bet I'm going to be really sore tomorrow. I must have hit my elbow on that bumper, too."

"Me, too. I think I've got an eyelash stuck in my eye."

I looked at him, and we both started laughing. Then we remembered why we were going past St. Bart's.

The school was closed on Saturday, of course, and the

gate was locked. There were no cars lined up in the pickup lane.

Pink was sober now. "Where did it happen, Joe?"

"Right up there. In front of that first apartment building. I was looking out that window, and the car eased up right about here."

"No blood on the sidewalk," Pink said.

"Of course not, you idiot. He wasn't stabbed, he was kidnapped."

"No black marks from his heels where they dragged him across the sidewalk. Hmm. There's the stub of a blue pencil in the gutter. It's a St. Bart's pencil."

"But anybody could have dropped it. No way to prove it belonged to Willie."

"Fingerprints," Pink said suddenly. "You think maybe? If it's his, he probably left fingerprints on it."

"Yeah. What have we got to protect it, in case we can get the cops to check it out? I threw away all my breakfast wrappings."

"So did I. There's a candy wrapper over here, maybe it'll work."

We retrieved it, and picked up the pencil in a way that wouldn't mess up any prints. And then it dawned on me. "What are the chances Willie's fingerprints are on file anywhere? He's a jerk, but he probably hasn't committed any serious crimes where he left prints behind."

Pink put the pencil in his pocket anyway. "Even Willie probably would have worn gloves to handle a murder weapon," he said.

We were trying to be funny, to keep it from being so

scary. But of course it wasn't *really* funny.

"I have to try not to think about Willie," I said as we headed toward home. "I wish I didn't have such a good imagination."

Pink, who always enjoys my stories but never comes up with any of his own, was intrigued. "What do you imagine about Willie?"

"Hog-tied and left in a closet, maybe. Or being tortured to tell them something—like the combination to his dad's safe, or where his dad keeps his cash. Or fastened to a cement block and dumped in the river. Even if he's okay—being fed, having a bed or a mattress to sleep on—he's gotta be scared, Pink."

"Yeah. He's gotta be scared," Pink agreed.

It wasn't quite late enough to go back to the deli for lunch, and I hoped my father had come home and talked to Willie's dad. So we went up to my place.

It was worse than it had been that morning.

I didn't know what all the people were doing, milling around. Mom was in the middle of them, explaining things, urging people to do what she needed. Ernie was there, setting up folding chairs in the music room. He looked at me with raised eyebrows.

"You come to help, sport?"

"No. Nobody's paying *me* time and a half. Or anything. Have you seen my father?"

"I'm supposed to pick him up around two." He set up one chair and reached for another.

"Do you know if Mr. Groves has tried to call again?"

"I'm just hired help, kid, nobody tells me anything.

You going to be hanging around in this madhouse, making yourself useful, or you got something planned this afternoon?"

I didn't want to get roped into hauling chairs upstairs. Or anything else. Surely they already had plenty of people to do everything that needed to be done.

"I've got plans," I told him, looking at Pink to make sure he knew I meant we would *make* plans.

In the hallway behind me, Mark passed by stuffing something interesting looking in his mouth.

"Where'd you get something to eat?" I demanded.

He lifted a fancy-looking pastry of some kind, with cream filling leaking out of it, which he caught with his tongue. "The bakery people are here. Stuff like this is in insulated containers, stacked back by the laundry area. If nobody sees you, you can lift a few."

Pink looked after Mark's retreating figure. "Looks good."

"Yeah. Let's give it a try," I agreed.

As we started to leave, Ernie called out, "Can you swipe a few for the paid help, too?"

"Go out the service entrance and pick up your own," I told him. "We'll be lucky to get away with ours."

"Ingrate," Ernie muttered as we left him.

We managed to liberate two confections apiece, and I hoped it wasn't Mom who emptied the containers later and saw how much of the top layer was missing.

"Better than deli stuff," Pink said, licking his fingers after the last one. "What now?"

"I guess we could go to a movie, after my father comes

home and I get a chance to talk to him. Right now, though, I want to check with Mom one more time and see if she's heard anything from Willie's dad."

My mother was directing the placement of some small potted trees. I rolled my eyes at Pink, who reached out to feel one of the leaves. "Real," he pronounced. "They're so perfect I thought sure they were artificial."

The doorbell rang.

Mom turned and opened the door, but it wasn't another one of the tradespeople she was expecting.

"Mrs. Bishop? I'm Detective O'Hara." He flashed some kind of ID at her. "I'd like to talk to you for a few minutes."

"I'm very busy right now, can it wait? Oh—is it about . . . ?" She swallowed at the same time I did, and stepped backward, allowing him to come in. "We can talk in the study, if you'll come this way."

He stepped into the foyer, dodging a guy with an empty hand truck whom Mom stopped by putting a hand on his sleeve.

"Please use the other elevator, back through the kitchen," she told him.

"Oh, sure, sorry," the guy said, and retreated through all the confusion.

The man who'd said he was a detective was staring at Pink and me. He was a medium-size guy, and very ordinary looking. Yet he sent prickles running along my spine.

"Is this Joe Bishop?" he asked.

The prickle turned icy. I licked my lips. "I'm Joe."

He didn't smile. "Be a good idea if you came along, too, son."

"Is Mr. Bishop here?" O'Hara asked as he stood aside for the rest of us to precede him into the study, where he closed the door.

"No, though I expect him in the next hour or so," Mom said nervously. "Is this about . . . the Groves boy?"

Detective O'Hara had pale blue eyes that were sharp enough to cut human flesh. As Pink said later, he almost checked to see if I was bleeding.

"If you'd all sit down, I'd like to ask some questions," he said, as if Mom hadn't spoken. "Anything discussed in this room is confidential. None of you are to repeat any of it elsewhere, with anyone."

This time it was Pink who was impaled on that cold blue gaze. "Are you one of the Bishop children, too?"

"Um, no, I'm Pink Murphy. Charles Murphy, actually. My dad's a vice president of the telephone company, Charlie Murphy. I know about Willie."

O'Hara might have been formed of steel.

"Who is it you're speaking of?"

"Willie Groves." Pink blushed. "The second," he offered unexpectedly. And then, when we all looked at him as he sank onto a couch, he added, "Willie's the third. His grandfather was the first."

"And what is it you know about Willie Groves?"

"I know he was kidnapped yesterday. Joey told me all about it. I didn't actually see it, but we went back to the school this morning, and we found what we think is his pencil in the gutter right where they grabbed him. We saved it for evidence. In case it has his fingerprints on it, you know. If they're on file anywhere."

Something suddenly occurred to me, and I cleared my throat. "I guess they wouldn't have to be on file, would they? I mean, you could get fingerprints in his room, on his things. If it's important to know if it's his pencil."

Pink dug the candy wrapper out of his pocket and handed it over. "We wrapped it up so we wouldn't smear any prints. It's a St. Bart's pencil, see, it says so right on the side of it. We all use them. This one was right where Willie was grabbed. We didn't find any of the rest of the stuff he dropped, so somebody else must have picked that up."

The detective opened the candy wrapper, glanced at the pencil, and dropped it into his own pocket. It wasn't Pink he responded to, but me. "What do you know about what happened to Willie yesterday?"

"All day? Or just after school?" I felt really flustered, and I didn't want to blow it just because I was a kid. This guy acted like he'd listen.

He hesitated for only a second. "Let's start with all day."

"Well, actually, it was day before yesterday that I gave him the nosebleed," I said.

My mother jerked and turned toward me, startled, but didn't interrupt.

"It was in PE," I explained quickly. "I accidentally hit him in the face with my elbow, and he bled a lot. I tried to apologize, but he was mad. He said he was going to get me for it."

The detective waited, and I couldn't tell what he thought.

"He didn't catch me after school that night. Ernie came before Willie had a chance to do anything."

"Ernie's our chauffeur," Mom said in a strained voice.

"So yesterday Willie bugged me all day, said he was going to beat me up. But one of the teachers—Mr. Soames, the math teacher—was talking to him after school, so I walked out the front door first." I felt myself getting hot, too, and wondered if I sounded to everybody like a hopeless wimp.

I wanted to look away from those light blue eyes, but I couldn't. "So you didn't see him after that?" he finally prompted.

"Oh, sure, I saw him. I went out the gate—there's a fence around St. Bart's—and the cars were lining up to pick up the kids, but I didn't see Ernie yet. So I started walking toward the corner, thinking he'd come along. Only he didn't—he was late. When he came along he said he'd had a fender bender and got held up—and so I walked down in front of that apartment house that's right next to the school. From there I looked back and saw that Willie had just come out the front door and was looking around." My face got hotter. "I didn't know what to do. Willie's . . . bigger than I am. I didn't especially want to get pulverized, and I figured if he had the weekend to cool off, maybe he'd forget it."

I couldn't read a thing in the detective's expression, but I imagined how contemptuous he must be feeling. I cleared my throat again. "Right then a delivery truck drove up, and when the driver buzzed the door at the apartment house, someone let him in. So before the door shut behind him, I . . . I went inside and waited for Willie to give up on me and leave." I wiped the sweat off my hands onto my pants. "Only he didn't. He came right up in front of the apartment. He didn't see through the window, but I could see out. And *his* car hadn't come, either, so Willie just stood there. And then *that* car came, the one with the kidnappers in it."

I wondered what it would take to change the man's facial expression, but I suppose he was used to hearing all kinds of fantastic or horrible things.

"Can you describe this car?" He reached into a breast pocket and brought out a small notebook and a pen, poised to write, all without taking his attention away from me.

"This year's model, a black Chrysler New Yorker. It had a monogram or something on the door, about this big. Gold and red and blue and green, bright enamel. The windows were too dark for me to see the driver, but when it stopped, a guy jumped out and grabbed Willie from behind and dragged him inside to the backseat, and I *did* see him. I tried telling everyone what had happened, but nobody believed me. I called 9-1-1, but the operator thought I was playing a practical joke, and he said I could get into trouble for making a false crime report—"

My mother was hearing some of this for the first time, and her mouth was hanging open a little bit.

"Tell him about—" Pink began, but Detective O'Hara silenced him with a glance.

"Did you get a license number on this car, son?"

"No, sir. By the time I got the door open, the car was

speeding away. Too far away for me to see."

"Did you get a good look at the person who pulled Willie into the car?"

"Yes, sir. Only for a few seconds, but I saw him. He wrapped an arm around Willie and pulled him backward, made him drop his books and stuff."

"Could you tell how tall he was?" The pen was waiting to write.

"Not exactly. Taller than Willie, who's a couple of inches taller than I am."

The blue eyes bored into mine. "As tall as I am?" He stood up to make it easier for me to judge.

"Maybe. Maybe a little taller."

"Do you remember his face?"

"Yes, but I don't know how to describe it. It was just . . . ordinary. He had black hair. And he was wearing an expensive-looking gold watch, and he had a gold earring, a little tiny one, in this ear." I touched myself to demonstrate.

"And did you go back to school to report this?"

"No. Ernie came right then, and I jumped in the car and told *him*. Only he didn't believe me. He thought I was making up a tall story."

For a moment I thought I glimpsed a flicker of something in his face, but it was gone so fast I couldn't be sure.

"Who else did you tell, besides the chauffeur, and the 9-1-1 operator?

"Pink," I said, gesturing at my friend. "I tried to tell Mom, but she was too busy. And my brother, Mark. He said I was full of crap. Sophie believed me—she's my sister. But there wasn't much *she* could do. And then Mom finally tried to call Willie's folks, but his mother was gone, and nobody would talk to her. My father placed a phone call yesterday evening to Mr. William Groves."

I think Mom felt the situation had all slipped away from her, and she didn't like it.

"Mr. Groves was not taking any phone calls when my husband attempted to talk to him," she said. She wasn't used to talking to police officers, and she wasn't comfortable with having one in our home. "And then Parnell—my husband—had to leave early this morning, so he wasn't home when Mr. Groves called back. I didn't know about it until after he'd already been told Parnell wasn't here." She waited, seeming to hold her breath.

Those stiletto eyes rested on me until I started to squirm.

"You said Willie dropped some 'stuff' when he was pulled into the car. Can you describe it?"

I hesitated. "School stuff. Uh . . . a math book, and a blue notebook. One of the ones they sell at school. A whole bunch of papers fell out and scattered around. A page with a red B– on it. That's all I can remember."

For a moment he was silent, before he turned to my mom. "I'd like Joe to come down to police headquarters and see if he can identify the man he saw. And also maybe work with a police artist in re-creating the man's face, if the mug shots don't pan out."

The study door opened and Mark stuck his head in, hesitating when he saw the group of us. "Uh, Mom, there's a caterer on the phone. There's some kind of problem. He needs to talk to you immediately."

"Oh, no!" she moaned, and stood up, glancing anxiously at Detective O'Hara. "Right now? You need Joey right now? Can it wait until my husband shows up?"

"Later this afternoon will be fine," the officer said. He handed her a card. "They'll be expecting him here."

"What's going on?" Mark demanded, looking from one face to the other. "Is this guy a *cop*?"

Nobody answered him, but Mark suddenly showed enlightenment anyway. "Holy cow, Joey, was it *true*? You really saw Willie *kidnapped*?"

"Everything being discussed here is strictly confidential," O'Hara said sharply, and Mark got the benefit of those glacial eyes.

"Yes, sir," Mark said. "I'll tell the caterer you're on your way, Mom."

They left us in the study, Pink and me. He let out a deep breath. "Wow! Just like on TV, Joey! Boy, wait'll we tell the other guys at school!"

"Not before they get Willie back," I warned him.

"Yeah, sure. Wow! I wonder if they'll interview you for the ten o'clock news?"

Chapter Seven

By the time we got as far as the kitchen, we found Mom on the phone again, saying, "Oh, no!" one more time. Then she said, "Yes, I'll hold," and I figured it was safe to interrupt.

"Mom, am I going to have to disappear into my room once the party starts?"

"That would be a good idea," she agreed. "Why don't you rent a video or two for the evening?"

"Okay. Would it be all right if Pink stays over, too? So it won't be so boring by myself?"

"Fine, if it's okay with his parents. Yes, Mr. Cardoni, I understand that. What can we do instead?"

She flipped a hand, dismissing me, and Pink and I went on back to my room to discuss what movie we wanted to see. Mark stuck his head out of his doorway as we passed it.

"Is it true, Joey? Was old Willie kidnapped?"

"I guess so. I told you that, and you said I was full of crap."

"Well, you usually are, so how did I know that for once you weren't making up some far-out story? Did that detective admit it, then?"

"He didn't admit anything. He didn't suggest anything. He didn't answer a single question any of us asked him. He just asked his own questions."

"He wanted details about the kidnapping, what Joe saw," Pink offered. "So it's gotta be true, doesn't it? Why else would he have come? And Joey's got to go down to the police station and look at mug books and maybe work with a police artist to come up with a sketch of the guy who grabbed Willie."

Mark whistled, impressed. "Does Dad know yet?"

"No. Mom asked if I could wait until he came home, to take me down there."

Mark grinned. "Boy, he's going to be irked. Mom, too. She was expecting him to help with something or other. And Ernie's hiding from her, I think, so she won't give him any more orders. He was grumbling about being hired to be a chauffeur, not an errand and delivery boy. Too bad I don't have my license yet, I could run the errands for them."

"No way is Mom going to let you drive in the city," I told him, pretty sure I was right. "Maybe next summer, if we go up to Grandma Charlotte's on the farm, they might let you drive there. On back country roads."

"You're just jealous because you can't drive for years yet. In or out of the city." He didn't want to talk about that. "Mug shot, huh? I wonder if they'll put the picture on TV and in the papers if you identify him? You know, if the guy finds out you saw him, and could identify him, he might come after you, Joey."

I hadn't thought of that, and I didn't like it much. "How would he find out?"

"I don't know. Reporters always manage to find out that kind of stuff, and they don't keep it a secret."

Pink didn't usually talk much when Mark was around, but he spoke up now. "Maybe he already knows, Joe. Maybe he was the guy who almost ran us down."

Mark had been heading back into his room, but he paused. "Somebody almost ran you down? When?"

"Just a little while ago," I said reluctantly. "He was just some creep in a cab who gunned it around a corner while we were trying to get across the street. You know how everybody drives in this city."

Mark acted like he was taking it seriously. "Funny coincidence, though, right? Just after you saw Willie kidnapped, and before you talked to the cops?"

Pink looked serious, too. "It was almost as if he intended to run over us, Joe. And he didn't stop."

"Does anybody ever stop, unless his own car is too damaged to run or he's pinned in by traffic?"

"He'd have got us, for sure, if that Camaro hadn't pulled out and got in his way," Pink said. "Maybe you better be careful."

It didn't seem likely, but the idea made me uneasy.

"Well," Mark said cheerfully, "watch your back, little brother."

I glared after him when he went back in his room. As soon as we'd closed my bedroom door, I demanded of

Pink, "You don't really believe what you said, do you? That the cab driver was trying to hit us? To hit *me?*"

"Could have been," Pink said. He flopped onto my bed. "It's true what Mark said, you know. If the kidnapper knew you saw him and could identify him . . ."

I scowled. He sounded as bad as my brother. "He didn't see me. I told you. And even if he had, he wouldn't have known who I was. The most he could possibly have seen was part of my face through a dirty window, for pete's sake."

"For the sake of argument," Pink suggested, "say somehow he *did* find out who you were. He *might* try to keep you from talking to anybody. Especially the police."

"But how would he have known where I was?"

"He could have been watching this apartment house. He could have followed us and been waiting for a chance at you."

"In a battered old taxi?" I scoffed, but my heart was beating faster.

"Maybe that's what he usually drives. Maybe he borrowed it from a friend. Maybe he rented it. More likely he stole it."

"But he was in an expensive late-model car when he kidnapped Willie."

"That might have been stolen, too. Or maybe he drives it for someone else. You know, he could be a chauffeur who had seen Willie at the school when he was picking up someone else's kid, and decided to pad his income with a little ransom money."

I didn't like the way Pink was coming up with logical

answers to everything. "But there's no way he could have known who I was," I persisted. "So everything else is a fairy tale."

Pink even had an answer to that. "Maybe Willie told him."

Exasperated, I wanted to kick him. "How could Willie tell him? He didn't see me, either!"

"Maybe not, but Willie was chasing you, wasn't he? The only reason he was in front of the door where you were hiding was that he was trying to find you to beat you up, and he told the kidnappers you'd disappeared right about there. They could have figured out you were hiding from Willie and saw *them*."

"*Why* would he have told them?"

"Because they tortured him, wanting to know why he was where he was instead of in front of the school, waiting to be picked up."

I didn't like Willie much, but I didn't want to think about possible torture. Making up such things in adventure stories was one thing; having it happen to anyone I knew was something else.

Another thing occurred to me. "How did they know they'd be able to kidnap him that long after school got out? If his usual ride had showed up on time, he'd have been gone before they got there."

"Didn't their maid say, when your mom first called the Groveses' apartment, that Willie was delayed in getting home because their car had been involved in a minor accident that held the driver up?"

"So what do you think? The kidnappers caused the

accident, and then rushed over to kidnap Willie? No kidding, Pink, I think you're nuts."

"What kind of a car was it that was involved with the Groveses' car?"

"How do I know?"

"Why don't we find out? Maybe it was a black Chrysler New Yorker."

"And maybe it wasn't. That car didn't have a mark on it that I could see, and if it did, it would make it easier to trace the car. They wouldn't want that. And how could they plot an accident and still be sure they'd get there in time to grab Willie, if they did it with the same car? In lots of accidents a cop comes, and even if he doesn't, the traffic gets snarled up so you don't know how long you'll be tied up."

Pink had been in my room plenty of times, but he looked around now as if he were seeing it for the first time. "How come you don't have a phone in here?"

"Because they don't think I'm old enough. Mark didn't get one until he was fifteen and kept tying up the phone Mom uses. Why do we need a phone?"

"To call somebody and see if we can find out what kind of car was involved with the Groveses' chauffeur's fender bender."

The whole thing sounded like one of my wildest fantasies, but between Mark and Pink, they'd made me nervous.

"If Willie's still missing, they probably aren't taking any phone calls. They're waiting to hear from the kidnappers," I said, feeling the need to deny everything Pink was suggesting.

"We won't know unless we try," he said, shrugging. "Let's see if Mark will let us use his phone."

Mark was more cooperative this time. "Sure." He started to hand me the phone, then hesitated. "You want me to call? My voice doesn't sound like a kid's, so maybe somebody will talk to me."

I hated to admit it, but he was right. Most of the time he sounded like a man on the phone. "Go ahead," I told him.

A few moments later, to my horror, and Pink's wide-eyed amazement, we heard him saying, "This is Officer Delaney, I'm working on the investigation. Would you give me the name of your chauffeur, please; we need to ask him a few questions. Oh, you did? Well, there are several of us working on the case, of course. Howard Patterson? And his home phone number? Yes, thank you. Perhaps you can save me a few minutes. Can you tell me about the minor accident Mr. Patterson was involved in, the day of the kidnapping?" Mark, looking at us, winked, obviously enjoying himself. "Certainly, I'll hold."

"What do you think you're doing?" I hissed. "Impersonating a police officer is a felony, isn't it?"

He covered the receiver with his free hand. "Cuts through a lot of hassle, and who's going to know the difference?" Then, removing his hand so that he could speak on the phone and lowering his voice as much as he could, "Yes, sir. Can you tell me if there was a police report made on the accident Mr. Patterson had that made him late to pick up Willie at school? No? I see. But the chauffeur did get the other driver's license number and ID? Insurance information? I see."

Mark was making a face now as if he really were an investigator. I'd forgotten how much he liked to act. I didn't see where playing a character in a play was that much different from making up stories for my own entertainment, but this wasn't the time to bring it up.

I lost track of the next few sentences he said, which was probably just as well. I was pretty sure he was telling more lies. When he finally thanked the speaker at the other end and hung up, he made a rueful face.

"That wasn't much help. Not much damage was done, and nobody was going to turn in an insurance claim and risk losing their coverage. There was a small amount of cash involved, handed over on the spot by the other driver, who admitted the accident was his fault. He was driving a standard yellow city cab."

"Like the one that nearly hit us," Pink said, just as I thought the same thing.

But again I was in denial. "There must be a million yellow cabs in this city. It wouldn't have to be the same one. Why didn't you ask what the other driver looked like?"

For once I caught Mark off base. "I didn't think of it," he conceded. "Well, I got the chauffeur's name and phone number. Let's call him, and if he isn't out driving the car maybe we can find out."

I suppose I could have stopped him from impersonating an officer this time, but for some reason I didn't. The real police weren't likely to tell us the answers even if they knew them. And it seemed important to know.

Mark had gotten into the swing of being an impersonator by this time, and he sounded like a real detective, running down clues. He wound up this call in triumph.

"Got it! The driver of the car that caused the fender bender with the Groveses' driver was a big guy with a Greek name the chauffeur couldn't remember off hand, dark hair, a strong, rather handsome man. Sound like the guy that snatched Willie?"

"No," I said. "Well, the guy was dark, but he wasn't especially good looking."

"So what does all of this give us?" Pink wanted to know.

"We didn't see the driver of the cab that nearly hit us, so that doesn't prove anything," I mused. "But we now know that it wasn't the kidnap car that kept the Groveses' chauffeur from getting to school on time."

There was a tap on the door, and Mom stuck her head in. "Mark, have you seen—oh, there you are, Joel. I want you to run down and give this list to Ernie, right away, before he leaves. He's at the service entrance."

"Okay. Come on, Pink. Then we'll check in with your mom and see if it's okay for you to spend the night."

"She won't care," Pink said, following me out into the hallway. "My sisters are having a slumber party tonight. If I'm gone, they can use my room, too."

On the way through the utility room we helped ourselves to a couple more pastries. They sure were good.

Ernie was in the alley, putting boxes in the trunk of the car. He slammed the lid and looked around as we came out of the building. "Ho. You off to more adventures?"

"No, just bringing you a list from Mom." I handed it over. He looked at it and sighed, then stuck it in his shirt pocket.

"Care to come along and help me pack this stuff?" he asked, reaching for the door handle.

"No, thanks," I said, and then I saw it. Parked in the alley, maybe twenty feet away.

The black New Yorker with the fancy emblem on the door.

Chapter Eight

They call it an alley, but it's really a one-way street behind our apartment building. On the other side of it is another big apartment complex. Parking isn't allowed except temporarily for loading and unloading, but there are usually vehicles there, using the service entrances. There are also Dumpsters, and the garbage trucks pass through to empty them. The cars belonging to residents are parked in an underground garage around the corner.

This afternoon Ernie was preparing to drive off on another errand before he picked up my father. I could tell he didn't want to do any more stuff for Mom, because if he was late picking up the boss, Father wouldn't like it much. Still, Ernie didn't dare insist on doing the errand later, not after Mom had indicated it was urgent.

There was a silver-colored Mercury Montego on our side of the alley, with no one in it. And another car on the other side where nobody was supposed to stop; the alley was to be kept clear so traffic could move on through. I probably wouldn't have paid any attention to the car if it hadn't been stopped in the wrong place.

My heart seemed to stop in my chest when I really *saw* it. A black Chrysler New Yorker, and I knew instantly that it was the car Willie had been dragged into.

I made some kind of gurgling sound, and Pink glanced at me, then sharpened his focus when he saw my expression.

"Joe? What's up?"

"That's it," I said, sounding hoarse. "That's the car, Pink."

He saw it then. "You sure?"

"Yeah." Breathing was an effort; I felt as if I were having to pull in air through a kind of plugged-up filter that wouldn't let me get enough.

"You guys change your minds?" Ernie said, sliding into the front of our car. "I could use some help."

My lips were numb. "That's the kidnap car. Right over there."

"Huh?" Ernie twisted around to look. "Come on, Joey, this is a hectic day. Give it a rest, okay?"

"It's true," Pink said, sounding squeaky the way he did when he was under stress. "It's not a story he made up this time. The cops were here and talked to him, and it's true. Willie Groves really is missing—"

I jabbed him in the ribs with an elbow. "Everything he said was supposed to be confidential, remember?"

Pink died in midsentence. "Oh, yeah. I forgot."

Ernie was sitting with the car door ajar, the window rolled down. "No kidding? The cops were here?"

No sense denying it now, I thought. Pink had let it

slip. "Yeah, but we're not supposed to talk about any of it."

"No kidding. I apologize, kid. I thought it was more of your usual baloney. What makes you think the car over there's the one the kidnappers used? There must be a couple thousand Chrysler New Yorkers in the city just like it. You said you didn't get a license number."

"That emblem on the door's not standard, though. Did you see anybody around that car?"

"Wasn't paying any attention," Ernie said. "I been busy. Want me to check it out, see if there's anything in it that might be significant? Get the license number?"

He reached over and got a little notebook out of the glove compartment, then brought a stubby pencil out of his shirt pocket and got out of the car.

"This is spooky," Pink muttered. "Shall we look at it up close, too?"

Ernie was already heading for the New Yorker, and Pink and I fell in behind him.

"What if the driver comes out and catches us?" I wondered aloud. "He can't be very far away."

He certainly wasn't. Before we were halfway there, the motor in the Chrysler roared to life, and the car jumped forward, right at us. It was those dark windows. The driver could see us, but we couldn't see him.

Ernie yelled something profane and dove sideways just in time. Pink and I threw ourselves behind the Dumpster on the opposite side of the alley.

I was aware of something stinging sharply, and of hitting my shoulder on the corner of the Dumpster, but I was too scared to give it much thought. I landed sprawled in some garbage that had been spilled outside the container, but I was still alive.

Pink was scrambling to his feet beside me, muttering his thoughts about the driver.

Ernie, too, was wiping something off his pants when we rejoined him. The black New Yorker was gone.

"Not much chance of getting a license number when the guy's trying to squash you flat," he said in disgust. "Looks like you were right, though, kid, about it being the same car. Why else would he try to kill all three of us?"

"I think he was trying to kill Joe," Pink said, wiping a hand across his mouth. "We just happened to be in the way, too."

I was shaking, and I couldn't stop. "Twice in only a couple of hours. The time with the taxi wasn't an accident either, was it?"

Ernie was scowling. "You mean somebody tried to run over you before?"

I explained, and his scowl deepened. "I suggest you kids get back inside and stay where there are lots of people. I gotta run, or I'm going to be late picking up your old man, and he'll be ticked."

He got in the car and drove away, leaving us standing in the alley.

I looked uncertainly at Pink. "Maybe it's not safe for you to hang around me. This guy doesn't care who he runs over, as long as I'm included."

"You think it was the same guy? Two different cars?" Pink asked. He was as shaken as I was.

"Probably. Although there was a driver *and* another

guy who grabbed Willie, so there must be at least two conspirators. And with the yellow cab, there might be a third. It doesn't matter much, does it? Come on, Ernie's right, let's get where there are people."

There were still plenty of them around. The florists had been allowed to come in the front way, but everybody else was coming and going in the service elevator. For once Mom wasn't on the phone, and she was smiling about the latest delivery.

"It looks beautiful," she was telling a slim young man who was on his way out. "Thank you so much."

She turned around and saw us. "Joel, for heaven's sake, what have you got all over yourself? And Pink, too? What have you been doing?"

"Diving into some crap to keep from being run over," I told her.

Her alarm made me wish I'd worded it differently, but the meaning would have been the same. "Joel! Are you all right?"

"Yeah." I explained. "Ernie said to come back up here and stay where there are people."

"I think I should call the police," Mom said at once, and herded us into the study where it was quiet enough to call.

"They're sending over an officer," she told us when she got off the phone. "Before he gets here, change your clothes. Don't throw these in the washer or anything," she added hastily, "because he may want to see them. I'm going to call your father and insist that he come home at once."

"Ernie's picking him up as soon as he gets the stuff on

your list," I told her. "I'll get Pink some of my clothes."

We found some more scrapes and bruises, none of them serious. But I couldn't stop shaking. Pink wasn't too relaxed, either.

We had to tell the whole story to Mark and Sophie. Sophie was horrified, Mark intrigued. "Wow! You aren't having to make up much of this one, are you? If he's tried twice to get you to shut you up, Joey, he'll probably try again." He said it almost with satisfaction.

Sophie was indignant. "You're a lot of help," she snapped. "Maybe something to drink would calm you both down," she said to Pink and me.

"I'm not allowed to drink anything alcoholic," Pink said. "Though maybe my folks would make an exception under the circumstances . . ."

"I wasn't talking alcoholic, silly," Sophie said. "Hot cocoa, maybe. That's what they gave all of us, that time John Abbott fell through the ice on the pond up at Grandma Charlotte's, and we all thought he'd drowned. Shall I make some?"

"Couldn't hurt," Pink agreed.

And I added, "Thanks, Soph."

"He must think you can identify him," Mark pressed. "Maybe he doesn't want you to find his picture in a mug book, so he wants to finish you off before you can look. Or before you can describe him for a police artist."

"How does he know I'm supposed to do that?" I demanded, whacking a palm on the top of my dresser. "The police visit was supposed to be secret!"

"He's probably got an inside person, feeding him

information. Maybe Junie's his spy," Mark said, laughing.

"Oh, shut up. We don't need any of your stupid remarks. You don't know what it feels like to wonder if somebody's trying to kill you."

"I wouldn't *wonder* at this point," Mark said. "I'd be sure."

"It's not funny," I said, and it wasn't. "Go on, get out of here."

He went, sort of chortling, and Pink rolled his eyes. "I'm glad I don't have an older brother."

"I'd be glad to get rid of this one," I said sourly, opening the closet door. "Here, this ought to fit you. Strip down, and we'll wash the crud off our hands before we get dressed again."

Pink was examining his arm. "What was it, anyway? It smells awful."

"Like somebody threw up there," I agreed as we headed for the bathroom.

It wasn't Detective O'Hara who came this time, but a Detective Phil Osbourne. He was thin, short, blond, with a wispy mustache.

He took all the information, said he'd want to talk to Ernie when he got back, and didn't give us any information about the kidnapping or what might be happening to Willie.

"He didn't act like it was any big deal," Pink observed after Mr. Osbourne had left.

"I suppose they have to deal with things like this all the time. Probably nothing much gets them excited. Let's have some more cocoa. I've almost stopped shaking, but I still feel cold."

"Like somebody's walking over your grave," Pink said solemnly.

For once I was glad when my father came home. It was somehow comforting to know that he was there, and that now he believed what I was saying.

Chapter Nine

"Can Pink go with Us to the police station?" I asked. I could tell by Pink's face that he was dying to go.

"This isn't a game, Joel," my father stated. "This is serious business, identifying a possible kidnapper."

"If Joe finds his picture in the mug book," Pink said eagerly, less intimidated by Father than I usually was, "I could look at the picture, too. I might recognize the guy. I mean, maybe he's somebody I've seen hanging around school or something."

To my surprise my father seemed to give this serious consideration. "All right. Come along. But if they won't allow you to stay with Joel, you'll have to sit in a waiting room."

"Great!" Pink said, raring to go.

Mom rested a hand on my shoulder as we started to leave the apartment. "Parnell, you won't let them . . . browbeat Joey, will you? I mean . . . he's only eleven."

"Why would they browbeat him?" Father asked impatiently. "All they want him to do is pick the man's picture out of their mug books, if he has a past criminal record that's on file. Calm down. If Joel needs a lawyer, I'll call in Dodds immediately. But Joel's a witness, not a suspect."

Mom still looked anxious. "And you'll be careful, won't you? I don't like the things that are happening. Joey could have been killed."

"Nobody's going to have the chance to do anything while he's with me," Father asserted. "Come on, let's ge going, so I can get back in time to greet the guests whe they arrive."

Ernie met us with the car at the front door. Sherman held the door for us, smiling at Pink and me after Father had gone past him. "Off on yet another adventure, are you?" he asked.

"To the police station," Pink said before I could stop him. I gave him a look, and Pink said, "Oh, I keep forgetting it's supposed to be a secret."

"The most interesting things are secret," Sherman said, his smile growing deeper. No doubt he thought we were making up a spy mission or some other kind of intrigue.

Father sat in the backseat, the way he always does. I joined him, and Pink sat up front with Ernie.

Father told him where to go, and Ernie said, "Yes, sir."

We slid out into traffic, which was heavy as usual. Father raised his voice to speak to Ernie. "Did that detective talk to you?"

"Yes, sir, he did. I couldn't tell him much. I didn't see the driver at all, didn't even realize there was anybody in the car until I was halfway across the alley. If I'd approached from the front, I could probably have seen his face. The windshield wasn't dark, of course, like the side windows. I wasn't all that sure Joey was right about it being the kidnap car, but the way the driver acted, I guess the kid knew what he was talking about."

"Had you seen the car in our alley before?"

"Not that I remember." Ernie glanced in the rearview mirror as he negotiated a corner. "Of course there are always vehicles out there. A few of them I've seen more than once. But the chauffeur-driven cars usually pick up passengers at the front door, not in the alley."

"Would you recognize the car if you saw it again?" There was a sharpness in Father's voice.

"Maybe. Joey noticed some kind of emblem on the door; I didn't get a very good look at it, though. I was too busy trying not to get run over."

"Call me—or the police—if you see it again."

"I will, sir, believe me. Do you want me to wait in front of the police station, Mr. Bishop? There's limited time parking, but probably if I explain what you're doing inside, I can get some leeway. Otherwise, I can drive around the block until you come out."

It was just like on TV. We went inside, and Father talked to a lady in uniform behind a desk. We only had to wait a few minutes before we were ushered into a small room. Nobody stopped Pink, so he came along, flushed and excited.

Everything was kind of a drab gray, and the floor was dirty, but there was a woman Junie's age with a bucket and a mop, cleaning it up. "Watch your step," she warned as we passed her.

In the little room was a table with a stack of big books on it and a couple of chairs. Another officer took one of the books off the pile and opened it in front of me. "Look at all the pictures carefully," he directed. "I'll be right through that door if you find the guy, okay?"

I didn't find him. After I finished with each book of mug shots, Pink looked through them, but neither of us saw anyone who looked familiar. I had hoped the kidnapper would be among the pictures, so they could go out and arrest him and rescue Willie. Willie must be pretty worried by now, I thought.

When we'd finished there, all of us disappointed, we were led up a broad flight of stairs and into another cubicle where we were introduced to Tony Lamont. He looked almost too young to be a cop. I thought he'd be drawing on a piece of paper, and I wondered how I was going to describe the kidnapper so he could be drawn. But Tony had a computer.

"Can you tell me the general shape of his face?" he asked as I took the chair beside him so I could see the screen, too.

Panic fluttered in my stomach. "Uh . . . I don't know. Just a regular face." I glanced toward Father, seated beside Pink across the room, but there was no help there. I was the only one who'd seen the kidnapper.

An image appeared on the computer screen. "Like this?" the operator asked. "Take it easy, think about it, don't rush."

I stared at the oval face. "No," I said finally. "It wasn't that round."

"More like this?" His fingers were quick on the keyboard, and the screen image shifted, narrowing, pulling in the cheeks.

"Maybe . . . maybe the guy's forehead wasn't that high."

It was fantastic what he could do with the computer. The hairline came down, and I began to have a prickling feeling along my spine. "Yeah, that's closer to it. And . . . I think the ears stuck out a little more." The ears moved, and I swallowed. "He was wearing an earring in the left ear."

"A stud? Just a little round one or a dangling one?"

"It was a circle, a tiny circle. Gold colored. No, that's too small. Yes, like that."

"How about the right ear?"

"I couldn't see that one. Or if I did, it didn't have an earring."

"How about his eyes? Like this?"

I studied the sketch. "Oh, wow, it's so hard . . . I only saw him for a few seconds, you know. And I was kind of in shock at what he was doing . . ."

"How about this?" The eyes, which seemed to be looking straight at me, became wider.

"I think . . . maybe a bit farther apart. His eyebrows were thick. Dark. Yeah, that . . . that's closer."

"How about his chin? Rounder? Pointed? Squarish?"

The face on the screen kept changing, little by little, and the kidnapper emerged. It was eerie, frightening, yet oddly satisfying, too, because by the time the police artist rested his hands on the keyboard, the kidnapper was there on the monitor. Pretty much the way I'd seen him in the few seconds before the door of the car slammed shut, hiding him behind dark glass.

Detective O'Hara walked into the room and peered at the sketch. "That look like the guy, son?"

"I think so." The fluttering took off again in my belly. "I think a person might recognize him from this. Do you think they'll be able to find him? It's an awfully big city."

"We'll find him," the detective said softly. "You said there was an emblem of some kind on the car door. Can you describe that?"

I tried, but the memory was so vague. "About this size, and maybe with an initial, or several initials in it. There was gold, and bright colors. Maybe around a capital C? Or an O? I don't know."

Pink piped up from his seat beside my father. "Have the kidnappers demanded a ransom?"

O'Hara glanced at him but didn't answer. "Run off a batch of these and get them distributed, all precincts."

The operator pushed the *print* key, and we watched as copies of the kidnapper's likeness began to spew out of the printer. The operator gathered them up, thanked me, and walked out of the room.

Pink came over to pick up one that had fallen on the floor.

"Ever seen him before?" I asked.

"Nope. But I'll notice if I do," he said. He folded the paper and put it in his pocket.

Ernie pulled up almost as soon as we reached the sidewalk. We showed him the picture. "This is the guy," I told him.

"No kidding. Good work, kid," he said as we headed for home.

I noticed he kept looking in the rearview mirror, more than usual, and I finally asked, "Is somebody following us?"

Ernie barked a laugh at this. "In this traffic, how could we tell?"

Nevertheless, Father turned around and scanned the cars behind us, and I thought maybe he was uneasy, too.

When we got home I showed the print to Sophie and Mark. They were both impressed. I got some Scotch tape and stuck it up on the inside of my bedroom door.

"Do you think they'll put it on the news?" Sophie asked.

"Yeah," Pink told her. "Probably."

"He only said to distribute it to all precincts," I remembered.

"That detective wouldn't say if they'd heard from the kidnappers. You know, a ransom note or anything like that," Pink observed. "Maybe the kidnapping is still a secret from everybody but the cops and the family. And Joe, of course, because he saw it happen."

Just in case, we tried a news station, but there was nothing yet. "It'll probably be on later," Pink guessed. "Are we gonna get a video or two to watch tonight, Joe?"

I stared at him. "You want to walk over to the video place to get them?"

"Oh. I forgot. I guess not. You think they've got this place staked out, watching for us to come out? You think that's why that car was in the alley?"

"Why would they think we'd go out the service exit?"

I said slowly, frowning. "I almost never go out that way. If they were watching anything, I should think it would be the front door."

"There's no place to park out there, though," Sophie pointed out. "Nobody could just sit in a car and watch for you in front."

True. But there was no logical reason for the kidnappers to think I'd go out into the alley.

"What was he doing out there, then?" Pink speculated. "Does he have some connection with this building?"

We couldn't think of any possibilities, but it seemed sinister that the kidnap car had been so close to us.

"Maybe Ernie could take you to the video place," Sophie said after a short silence. "I don't think he's gone off duty yet."

Pink perked up. "Yeah, let's see if he can! Otherwise, we're going to be stuck with what's on regular TV, and there isn't much scheduled. I already looked."

Mom, for once, was sitting down in the kitchen, having a cup of tea. I asked about Ernie.

"No, he hasn't gone yet. He's going to stick around until the caterers have come—they're due soon—in case he needs to do anything else. There's no reason why he can't leave long enough for you to get your videos. Tell him to be careful, though, you hear?" She hesitated. "On second thought, maybe it would be better if he took Mark to pick out something for you. I kind of hate to let you out of my sight until this kidnapping thing's been resolved."

"Mom! You know the kind of junk Mark will pick out! If Pink and I go with Ernie, nothing's going to happen!"

Even as I said it, I began to doubt the truth of that, but it was true that Mark wasn't a reliable movie picker. Once when I had to stay home with a strep throat, he brought me old Shirley Temple movies and Rin-Tin-Tin.

Mom sighed. "Well, just tell Ernie to be careful."

"Once they run that sketch on TV," Pink said, "there won't be any reason to try to get at Joey, will there? I mean, why else would they try to run over him except to shut him up? Keep him from identifying the guy?"

"The whole thing makes me very nervous," Mom admitted. "But your father says we can't wrap you in cotton and keep you locked up forever. So tell Ernie to be extra careful."

I didn't need to tell Ernie. He'd been right alongside of Pink and me when the car in the alley had nearly hit us, and nobody doubted it was *me* the driver had been aiming at.

I didn't think I was going to be scared to go out in the alley, but at the last minute, before I pushed open the door, my mouth got dry. What if the kidnapper was out there again?

He wasn't, though. Ernie was lounging in the front seat of our car, cleaning his fingernails with his jackknife, and two catering vans were just pulling in behind him.

We held the door open for the caterers. They had all kinds of containers, hot and cold, apparently. I was beginning to get hungry again, but there was no way to snitch anything here with four people from the caterers keeping an eye on things.

Ernie didn't mind going to get the videos. It was only four blocks away. "Been a long day, and I'm going to pick up Alice right after I finish," he said as we piled in the backseat. "Going over to Ma's for a spaghetti dinner. My ma makes the best spaghetti I ever ate."

He flexed an arm, keeping one hand on the wheel as he put the car in gear. "That's where all this muscle came from."

There was no sign of the New Yorker, nor anybody who looked like the guy in the picture. "I'll circle the block," Ernie said. "Otherwise I'll get ticketed for double parking. Make it quick, okay?"

To be on the safe side, in case one of the movies wasn't as good as we hoped it would be, we picked out four videos. The store was crowded, and we had to wait to check them out. Pink offered to step outside and flag Ernie down the next time he came around the block while I finished making out the slips.

I had almost reached the front door when Pink pushed in, his face so pale his freckles stood out like speckles of rusty paint.

"What's the matter?" I demanded, clutching my stack of videos.

"I just saw him, Joe! He just walked past on the sidewalk!"

"Who?" I asked stupidly, glancing past him through the glass doors to where pedestrians were hurrying past.

"Him!" Pink gasped. "The guy with the earring!"

Chapter Ten

I felt as if I'd grown roots. I didn't move until someone jostled me from behind. "Excuse me," a guy said impatiently, and I sucked in a breath and stepped aside, feeling numb.

"Are you sure?" I asked.

"Yes! He's just like the picture the police artist made! Come on, Joey, we've got to find out where he goes!"

Out on the street Pink pointed to a figure half a block away. "See him? The guy in the dark blue jacket!"

"I can't tell from here. I can't see his face, or even the earring. Where's Ernie? Maybe we can follow him," I said.

But Ernie, after a startled look, pointed out, "I can't follow him without going around the block first to turn around."

"Well, then, do it!" I cried. "We're going to lose him!"

Ernie followed orders, but it was clear he thought it was a waste of time. "Even if it's him, he's long gone. Probably it's a stranger, though. There are plenty of guys walking around with earrings."

"I saw him face-to-face," Pink insisted as we rounded the last corner and headed back toward home, in the direction the man had taken. "He looked just like the sketch, Joe, he really did!"

Ernie was driving as slowly as he could without the traffic running right over us. "What was he wearing?"

"Dark pants, a dark blue jacket. And he was carrying a bag of groceries or something. Yeah, groceries. There was one of those long loaves of bread sticking out of the top of it, like the ones you get from the French bakery. That's all I saw. But I don't see anybody like that now." His voice was heavy with disappointment.

If Pink had really seen the guy, he had disappeared somewhere. Vanished into a side street or into a building.

I slumped back in the seat when Ernie pulled into our alley. The caterer's vans were still there, but nobody was around.

"Do you think we should report it to the police?" Pink asked as we got out of the car.

"If you're sure it was him, yeah. They could be watching the area where you saw him, maybe."

I didn't have to use my key to go in the service entrance. The door had been propped open with a cardboard carton, strictly against the rules, but we left it that way anyhow. Several guys in white shirts, black pants, and bow ties, with the caterer's name on their black vests, came out of the elevator, carrying containers back to their vans. I heard Ernie's voice behind us, in the alley, as they went on through.

"I've got orders to help any way I can. What do you want me to move?"

"You getting hungry?" Pink asked as the elevator took us upward.

"Yeah. Starving. We better call the cops first thing, though. Or tell my father, and let him do it."

Father inspected our faces the way he'd always done when I told him anything he didn't immediately accept, then nodded briefly. "All right. I'll report this. We'll have guests arriving within the hour, so get whatever you're going to need out of the kitchen, and stay out of sight the rest of the evening," he ordered.

After he'd headed for the phone in his study, we looked around the kitchen. "Do we dare eat any of this stuff?" Pink asked hopefully.

Sophie came through the doorway in time to hear him.

"Mom said we could heat TV dinners, but there's so much food here nobody's going to miss the little bit we'll eat. Mark already took a plateful to his room. Let's get what we want and leave before Mom comes back to check."

There were sandwiches that looked like pinwheels; I sampled one to make sure it was as tasty as it looked, then piled half a dozen of them on a plate.

"Wow, these are good," Pink said, helping himself to some little individual quiches and lifting the lid off a pot of meatballs. We made a quick pass around all the stuff that was heating in various places and packed in containers, poked into the refrigerated foods, and heaped up enough to last us for a few hours, anyway. Then we all trooped back to my bedroom, where Father found us a few minutes later.

"They said if the man was carrying groceries, he probably lives in the area. Every officer on patrol will know what he looks like."

"Do you think that means that they're hiding Willie close by?" Pink asked, licking juice from the meatballs off his lips.

"Possibly." Father looked over what we were eating without comment. "No doubt we'll find out before long, when they rescue the boy. Now remember, your mother has worked hard to make this party a success, and it's important for me in a business sense, so don't disrupt it. Don't go out anywhere. There's no sense in putting yourself in further danger, Joel."

After he'd gone we settled down on the bed with our food. "Which movie are we going to watch first?" Pink wanted to know.

"Before you start, maybe we could find a newscast," Sophie proposed. "We could see if they show that sketch Joey told them how to make."

So we turned on the TV and flipped channels until we found a newscast. We had to sit through stuff about Congress and some big warehouse fire and a gazillion commercials. There was no reproduction of the sketch the police artist had made.

I was disappointed, but I hoped that meant they had some other way of catching up with the kidnappers.

Willie had been a bully, angry with me because of an

accident, nothing I did on purpose. He'd felt he could threaten me because he was taller and heavier and he knew he could push me around.

Now someone was pushing *him* around. Scaring him. Maybe hurting him. I hoped they weren't torturing him, that they wouldn't kill him, even. I hoped if they'd demanded a ransom that his dad could come up with the money. But I couldn't help hoping, too, that this experience would change Willie's personality for the better.

I wondered if he'd still be mad at me after he was rescued. *If* he was rescued.

We had just started the first video—which promised adventure, romance, and spectacular special effects—when Mark came in without knocking. Typical. Mark never knocked, at least not until he was already halfway in.

"Hey, Sophie, I need you to run an errand. Go downstairs to Andy's and bring up a math book, will you? I forgot mine, and we've got a test coming up Monday."

Sophie bit off half a miniature quiche before she asked, "Why don't you go after it yourself?"

"Because I'm in the middle of this really exciting show, live, and I don't want to miss any of it. His folks are taking everybody out for the evening in a few minutes, so I can't wait."

"If I go, I'll miss part of *my* movie," Sophie objected.

"Yours is a video. They can wait for you for a minute," Mark said. "Come on, I have to get back."

"I don't think so," Sophie told him. "My supper's hot right now, and besides, I'm nervous about running around while all this stuff about Willie is going on."

Mark scowled at her and turned his attention to me. "You go, then, Joey. It'll only take you a few minutes. I'll make it worth your while."

"How worth my while?" I demanded. I knew they'd restart *our* movie when I got back.

Mark dug into his pocket and dug out a crumpled bill. "Here, go on. It'll only take you five minutes. My show's coming back on, I gotta go."

He shoved the money at me and took off without waiting for my answer.

"Are you going to do it?" Sophie asked.

I stared at the bill in my hand. "Well, wait for me to get back to watch our movie, okay?" I took time for a few bites of the meatballs before they were completely cold.

Sophie didn't look happy. "Daddy said you weren't to go out anywhere. Just in case." She didn't specify just in case what, but she didn't have to.

"He meant outside the building. What could happen here inside the building? A minute in the elevator each way, another minute for Andy to answer his door and hand over the book. If I don't go, I'll have to give the money back." Besides having Mark mad at me, I thought. He always thought everybody else should do what he wanted, and it annoyed him if we didn't go along with him.

"I'll be right back," I decided, setting my plate aside. "If you guys go after dessert before the party starts, get me some, okay?"

Nobody paid any attention to me when I walked through the apartment toward the hall and the elevator.

The caterers were apparently leaving, except for a few people sticking around to serve. Junie was doing something last minute in the kitchen, and I could hear Mom's voice somewhere out of my sight.

I would be glad when things got back to normal. I hoped us kids wouldn't have to help with the cleanup when it was all over. Poor Junie needed the overtime, anyway.

The elevator was on our level, so I didn't have to wait. I zipped down to the sixth floor, got the math book, and then had to punch the button to get the elevator back; it had gone on down to the lobby.

When it came, the doors slid open, and I saw that there were two people already in it. Nothing about them registered until I had gotten on and the doors closed behind me.

Then I glanced around and saw him.

Two feet away, carrying a paper sack again, this time with a carton of orange juice sticking out of it.

The guy with the earring.

Chapter Eleven

The dinosaurs must have felt like this when the glaciers swept over them, burying them in ice, cutting off their oxygen.

The elevator was moving, silently as always. If I'd been able to breathe, I could have heard myself doing it.

I couldn't really think, then, but I remembered later.

There were two men. One was tall and rather slim, dressed in a blue suit with a red and white tie. He was carrying a briefcase.

The other one was not as tall, but more muscular, in a dark blue jacket. I'd done a good job of describing him for the police artist, because he looked a lot like the picture produced on the computer.

My chest had begun to ache. I had to draw in some air, but I couldn't do it. I stared straight ahead, not looking at the men. I could see the floors flipping by, and I prayed the two would get off before the elevator reached our apartment on the top floor.

Sometimes praying helps a lot. This time it didn't,

though for a moment I had hope. The men had pushed the button for the floor below ours, and the elevator came to a stop. The doors slid open, and I thought they were going to get off and I was going to be safe.

Then my fingers, gone numb in shock, forgot to hang on to the math book I was carrying. It slid out of my hand and landed with a thump on the floor of the elevator.

Both men swiveled to look at me.

The sack the nearest one was carrying split down the side as he turned, spilling stuff onto the floor. A package of chips landed on my foot, a couple of TV dinners—Mexican—skidded toward the front of the elevator. The juice container split and began to leak.

The elevator doors opened, but the men didn't get off. Instead they were staring at me.

"It's him!" the taller one said. "It's that Bishop kid!"

The elevator doors decided nobody was getting off, so they closed before anybody moved to stop them, and we rose the rest of the way to our floor, where they opened again.

I finally managed to get a gulp of air, and I lurched forward, actually getting a foot into the hallway before the men moved.

"Stop him!" one of them cried, and a hand grabbed the back of my shirt.

I twisted, desperate now to reach our door and safety. I heard my shirt rip, and for an instant I was moving again. Then he got a solid grip on my arm and wrestled me to the floor. With his weight on top of me, I didn't have a chance. I couldn't even gather enough wits to pray that someone would come out of our apartment, that something would happen to save me.

"Hurry up, get him in the elevator," one of the men said, and I was hauled backward in a way that almost strangled me. I was trying to yell for help, but it came out a squawk that wouldn't have carried very far.

I was slammed against the rear wall of the elevator as the doors came shut, and we dropped downward. Tears of pain and fear formed in my eyes.

"Hurry up," the tall one said as we returned to their floor. "If someone calls for the elevator, we don't want anyone to have noticed where it's coming from, when they start looking for him."

There were two apartments on this floor. They hauled me out of the elevator, unlocked the door into one of them, and jerked me roughly inside.

"Move," the shorter one said, and the door closed behind us.

If terror really killed people, I'd have died right there.

"What are we going to do with him?" the one with the earring demanded, shoving me along through the foyer and into a living room beyond. He was propelling me fast enough so that when he finally let go, I fell onto a couch.

"I know what I'd like to do with him." The tall one stood over me, pursing his lips. "It was a good plan, and everything was going just the way it was supposed to, until this nosy brat stepped in."

"We'll have to shut him up."

I flinched. I hoped shutting me up didn't mean permanently.

"We don't have time to deal with him now. Lock him up. We'll talk about what to do with him later."

"With the other kid? Or by himself?"

"What difference does it make? They can't do anything behind locked doors." The tall one seemed to be the boss. He had picked up the things that fell out of the sack, and he turned away with them. "I'll stash this stuff in the kitchen, and then we'd better get ready to go."

The other kid. That registered. If I'd had any doubts that they were the ones who'd kidnapped Willie, I didn't now.

I was dragged to my feet and urged across the room and into a hallway. The guy with the earring produced a key and unlocked a door, and I was thrown inside, on my knees. I heard the lock clicking shut behind me.

"Bishop?" The voice was familiar, incredulous.

I raised my head and met Willie's eyes. He was sprawled out on the bed, and he sat up.

"What are you doing here?"

"They kidnapped me, too, I guess. So I couldn't tell anybody about them." I got up and rubbed the place on my arm where it had been twisted. "Are you okay?"

"If you call being locked up this way okay, I guess so," Willie said. He didn't seem quite as big as he had when I'd last seen him at school.

I licked my lips and eased onto one corner of the bed, facing him. "I imagined you being tortured or something, to make you talk."

He stared at me as if I were an idiot. "Talk about what?"

"I don't know. The combination to your dad's safe, maybe."

"I don't know the combination to my dad's safe. How come they kidnapped *you*? Are they going into this business wholesale or what?"

"I don't think so," I decided. "I think it's because I saw them kidnap you, and then I described the one with the earring for the police—"

He sat up straighter, dropping one foot to the floor. "You did? Where were you?"

I explained to him, feeling kind of foolish. If I hadn't run away from him and hidden in the foyer of that apartment house, they'd never have been able to kidnap either one of us. Well, maybe they'd have still snatched Willie, but *I* wouldn't be here now.

"You said the police. Are they looking for me?" he asked eagerly.

He didn't include *me*, I noticed. "I guess so. They didn't tell us anything, but I described the guy I saw, the one with the earring, and they made a computer picture. It hasn't been on TV yet, but it was distributed to the cops, so they know what one of them looks like."

"Did they have my picture, too?" Willie demanded.

"No. Just the kidnapper's. Or maybe the cops got your picture from your family."

He scowled. "Why don't they have my picture in the paper? I'm the one who's missing!"

"Who knows why the cops do anything? I don't think

they've made it public that you've been kidnapped. Probably the kidnappers threatened your dad if the news gets out before they collect the ransom."

"Then if the cops are already looking for them, how come they needed to kidnap *you?*"

"Because I met them in the elevator in my own building. I don't suppose they want me to report that they're here. Why *are* they here? This building is full of families of businesspeople, not crooks."

Willie gazed at me for a moment, then decided to reveal his superior knowledge. "The man who lives here, Mr. Zoulas, is in Paris for the rest of the month. One of the kidnappers—the tall one who dresses in suits—is a personal secretary for him. His name is Studen. The other one, Tedesco, is somebody's chauffeur. I think he used to work for Mr. Zoulas, but he got fired. Now he drives for a Mrs. Civen. She's gone, too, to Miami. Between them, they have the use of this apartment for a couple of weeks and longer than that for Mrs. Civen's car. So they decided it would be a good time to kidnap some rich kid, for the ransom, and stash him here where nobody would think to look. Until the ransom's paid, that is."

"But then what? Everybody knows what they look like," I objected. "You would know even if I hadn't seen that what's-his-name, Tedesco? So how can they let you go?"

Willie stared at me as if he'd never thought of this possibility. "My dad will pay the money, and then they have to let me go," he stated.

"Why will they? What are they going to do, take you

home so you can tell the police everything and they can catch the kidnappers? So you can swear in court they're the ones who did it, so they'll be sent to prison forever? Why would they do that?" Seeing that he still didn't quite grasp what I was getting at, I added, "As far as I know, there aren't any rules for kidnappers. They do whatever they think they can get away with. They do expect to get away with this, don't they? At the very least, they'll need time to escape, out of the country, maybe, after they've collected the ransom. Turning you loose will make it harder for them, so why should they do it?"

It was clear from Willie's face that I'd brought up some unwelcome ideas. "They said all I had to do was sit tight until my dad forks over the money, and then I'd be all right."

"And you believed whatever they said? You think guys who would kidnap a kid and extort money from his family would stop at telling a lie or two to keep you quiet?"

He was frowning deeply now. "If they're not going to turn me loose, what are they going to do with me?"

"And with me," I reminded him. "I'm here, too. I don't know, but I'm sure they don't want to be caught. What if your father can't pay the ransom they're asking for?"

"He can pay it. I'm his only son, and he'll pay whatever they ask for."

"Well, I don't know if my father will get a ransom demand, too, or not. And I don't know how he'd raise a lot of cash on a Saturday. Or maybe they don't intend to ask for money for me. Maybe . . ." I stopped, swallowed, and realized I was scaring myself as much as I was scaring him.

"Maybe what?" Willie asked with a tremor in his voice.

"Maybe they don't intend ever to send us home . . . alive."

Chapter Twelve

Willie sat very still and got redder and redder. Then all the color washed out of his face and he was so pale I wondered if he was going to faint. I felt like fainting myself.

What if the kidnappers *didn't* intend to let us go? Ever?

We looked at each other, not speaking for a minute or so.

It was a nice room. As nice as our apartment. The other rooms had been nice, too. A comfortable home. I began to remember things I'd seen as I passed through the living room.

A Mr. Zoulas lived here, but he was in Paris now. He thought he could trust his secretary, the man called Studen, and he'd left his home for the man to take care of. Mr. Zoulas collected things: paintings, and different kinds of wood carvings that had maybe come from Africa and India, and books. He had hundreds of books.

There were some of his collected items in here. A bookcase that held quite a few books, and an elephant carved from some kind of dark glossy wood, and a running horse with a flowing mane, of an even darker wood.

There was a telephone jack, but no phone.

Willie saw me looking at it, and finally spoke. "They took it away. So I couldn't call for help, of course."

"Yeah. Do they ever give you a chance to get out of this room? There must be another phone somewhere."

"There is, because I've heard one ring. But the only place they've let me go is to the bathroom." He jerked a thumb toward a door across the room.

"What's in there? Anything useful?" I got up and walked over to check it out. Some people had phones in their bathrooms, but this place didn't. Just the standard kind of things people put in their guest bathrooms. I tried the door into the hallway, but it was locked.

Willie had come to stand behind me in the doorway. "Nothing to help me escape," he said.

"Have they fed you?" I turned around to face him.

"Sure. Mostly junk my mom won't let me eat. I don't think either of them can cook."

"At least you're not going hungry. I imagined you going hungry."

"And being tortured. You said you thought about me being tortured." He wasn't looking all that friendly. "How come you imagined me being tortured?"

"It just seemed like the kind of thing kidnappers might do. It was pretty scary, watching you get dragged into that car, and I didn't know what to do about it."

"You could have given the police the license number."

"I didn't see it. I didn't get outside until the car was too far away." Facing in a different direction, I saw something else. "You've got books and a TV in here. That's better than a dungeon."

"Where would anybody find a dungeon in a modern city?" Willie said. "The books are all stupid. About hydraulic mining and archaeology and medical research. Who wants to read about that kind of stuff?"

"They might be interesting," I observed, thinking that maybe it was Willie who was stupid, not the books. My father had all kinds of books on technical things in his study, and I'd looked at some of them.

Willie walked over and turned on the TV. "I can't believe there's nothing on TV about me. Maybe you didn't have it on the right station."

I stood watching while he changed channels, looking for a newscast. The only one he could find was mostly international news and football scores. No police sketch of the man named Tedesco.

I sat down in the only easy chair in the room, wondering if they'd missed me yet at home. How long would Sophie and Pink wait for me to come back? Or would it be Mark who got annoyed because I hadn't brought the math book yet?

Where was the math book? I'd dropped it in the elevator. Had the man named Studen picked it up, or was it still there, where someone would find it?

It would be Sophie, I decided, who'd get worried enough to go to Mom and Father and report that I was missing. It would probably spoil the party. My mother would be very upset. I wasn't sure if my father would be upset or angry. Probably a little of each.

I felt sorry for Mom because she'd worked hard to make it a good party. What would they do with all that food if they had to send the guests home?

Mark says I'm the kind of person who doesn't know when to keep quiet. Maybe this was one of those times, but I felt compelled to talk.

"I've been gone long enough so someone's sure to miss me by now," I said. "My father told me not to go outside, and my brother and sister and Pink know I was only going down to the sixth floor to get Mark a math book. So maybe they'll realize I'm still in the building. Maybe they'll check out the whole place and find us."

"All anybody'd have to do," Willie pointed out, "is deny we were in the apartment. Unless they get warrants for every apartment in the building, they can't get in and look around."

I scrutinized the ordinary furnishings of the room. "What have you tried so far?"

"Yelling, when they first grabbed me. So they gagged me when they brought me up in the service elevator, in case somebody was around. They locked me in here with a key, but they didn't leave it in the lock. And they haven't given me a newspaper so I could push it under the door and knock a key out onto it, to pull it back to me. The carpet's right at the bottom of the door, so that wouldn't have worked anyway. And I think at least one of them's been here all the time, keeping an eye on me."

"If there's only one man here, and we could get him to open the door for some reason, maybe the two of us could jump him," I suggested.

"Tedesco, the one with the earring, is really strong," Willie said. "I doubt if we could overpower him. If he comes in, though, we can try it."

"We need to attract attention from someone else. Somehow," I said.

"Like building a fire in the wastebasket? Making a lot of smoke? I thought of that. Except I don't have any matches. And I'd probably die of smoke inhalation before anyone even noticed what was going on."

"I wonder how long it would take," I said thoughtfully, "if we filled the bathtub and let it run over, before it leaked through the ceiling and somebody noticed it on the next floor down? They'd investigate that, for sure."

"It would probably run under the door into the hallway before it went through the floor. They'd come and stop us. Studen is using the room right next to this one, so he'd be down the hallway often enough to catch us."

"Mark says I'm always being irritating, to get attention." I walked to the window and looked out.

"I'll testify to that," Willie agreed.

I turned my head to look at him, unable to decide if he was looking really mean or not. "I never meant to hit you in the nose and make it bleed," I told him.

"It hurt," Willie said. "It hurt a lot."

"You still want to beat me up?" I asked.

"Not until after we get out of here," Willie conceded. And then, at the same time, we both started to laugh.

It didn't last long, though, because there was nothing funny about our predicament. I was afraid that what I'd suggested was true; even if Mr. Groves paid a big ransom, they wouldn't let us go for fear it would lessen their chances to get away.

"Well," I said finally, "if we can't figure a way to get out, we'll have to figure a way to get someone else to come in. Forcibly, if they have to. We've ruled out setting a fire or causing a flood. So what else is there?"

"You're the one with the imagination. I remember that tall story you told Mr. Epperson about what happened to your essay on Shakespeare. I thought he was going to give you an A just for being so inventive, even if he didn't believe you. So *you* tell *me*."

I looked out the window again. "It just happens that I really did leave the paper on the kitchen table, and it stuck to the bottom of that pan of cinnamon rolls Junie was making, and she put it in the oven and it caught fire. And when I rewrote it, he marked it down to a B because it was a day late." I pressed my face against the glass. "There are hundreds of people down there. They'd probably help us if they knew about us."

"The window won't open. I tried it," Willie said.

"How about the one in the bathroom? Is that sealed shut, too?"

"Yes. I tried to break it by hammering on it with the end of a plunger I found under the sink in the bathroom, but the glass wouldn't break. And Tedesco heard me banging and came and took away the plunger."

"So we can't drop notes on anybody below." I stared across the street, at the next apartment building. It was a Saturday night. Many of the windows were dark. People had gone out to dinner or the movies or to a concert or something.

Yet there were a few lights on. Directly across from us an old lady sat in the window. Not looking at us, but down at something on a table in front of her, maybe doing a crossword puzzle. I waved my hands around, but she didn't look up. People in the city don't pay much attention to what's going on in windows across the street.

One level down, a guy in his undershirt looked as if he might be watching television. He had a can in one hand, and as I watched he lifted it to take a swig.

Two windows over, on that same level, a young man was working at a computer. He had a can beside him, too.

None of them so much as glanced my way.

If only one of our own windows was visible from here! Of course Mark and Sophie and Pink might not even be in the rooms on this side of the building now; if everybody had missed me, they might be in a panic, trying to find me.

Far below, a police car passed the intersection, sandwiched between yellow taxis. The police officer in it had probably seen Tedesco's picture, probably knew Willie had been kidnapped, maybe by this time even knew that I had disappeared.

If I were writing this as a story, I'd have figured out a way to escape.

And then I thought of something.

"Is there a mirror in the bathroom?"

"One on the front of the medicine chest," Willie offered. "What good will that do us?"

"Is it one we could pry off? Take screws out of the door or something, and get it apart so we could bring the mirror part in here? My mom used to say that when I was four I could take anything apart, including things she'd just told me didn't *come* apart. I took all the doohickeys off the backs of clocks for years, until I finally got shocked taking apart an electric digital. I didn't trust clocks after that."

Willie went into the bathroom and I followed him. He was inspecting the mirror on the medicine chest door. "I don't see how we'd get it apart. It takes a Phillips screwdriver even to get the hinges off the door, and the mirror seems to be made right into the door before they put the pieces of it together."

We looked around for something to use as a screwdriver, and found nothing that would work even on an ordinary screw.

In the apartment beyond the bathroom door, the telephone rang.

We stopped moving, then ran to put our ears against the door, hoping to be able to hear something. There was a murmuring of a man's voice, but we couldn't make out the words.

Frustrated, Willie and I stared at each other.

How much time did we have? They might get the ransom money tonight, or surely by tomorrow; then what would they do with us?

Willie must have been thinking the same thing. "They could just leave us locked in here, I suppose. Mr. Zoulas would find our bodies when he comes back from Paris."

"They might leave something for us to eat," I said, but I didn't believe it, and I could tell by Willie's face that he didn't believe it, either.

Somewhere a door closed audibly.

Were we alone in the apartment now, or had one of them stayed behind to guard us against escape?

We stopped breathing to listen.

Chapter Thirteen

Out in the living room something thumped.

So much for the hope that we were alone. If there was nobody to stop us, we might be able to break down a door, or take out the hinges if we could improvise a tool to do it. But that would make enough noise to bring the remaining kidnapper down on us.

Then there was a murmur of voices, almost—but not quite—understandable. So there were still two of them here.

"I wish we could hear what they're talking about," Willie said, grinding his teeth in frustration. "It's never quite loud enough."

Without explaining, because I wanted to hear, too, I took the water glass that sat beside the sink. I pressed the open top of it against the door, then leaned my ear against the bottom.

"Can you hear better?" Willie hissed, and I motioned for him to be quiet. When he shut up, I could actually make out a few words.

"—picking up the ransom now."

Willie could tell from my face that I'd heard something significant. He leaned closer, as if he, too, might be able to hear something, even without the conducting glass.

And then we lucked out, in a way. Because the two men who were talking were coming along the hallway, and their voices became clearer. We could both hear them.

"Stupid," one of them was saying. "Why did you bring him here?" The voice was vaguely familiar, though I didn't immediately place it.

"Because it was the closest and the easiest," the second voice responded with irritation.

"Tedesco," Willie whispered, identifying the second speaker.

"And the most dangerous," the first man replied. "Now he'll have to be taken care of, too."

Me? I wondered. Were they talking about me? What did they mean by *taken care of*?

"If everything goes all right, Studen should be back here in half an hour, an hour at the most. I gotta clear out the rest of our stuff, and we're ready to go." Their voices faded out then as they either walked past our door or entered one of the other rooms.

I straightened up and took the glass away from the door. "I always wondered if that really worked, using a glass to amplify sound," I said. I was trying to sound cool, but I was shaking, so I don't think I fooled Willie.

Willie had gone pale. He leaned against the wall, and I decided he was pretty shaky, too. When his voice came out in a whisper, I didn't know if he was trying to be very quiet, or if he felt too weak to speak any louder.

"Studen's gone after the ransom," he said. "What if . . . what if my dad couldn't get it together after all?"

"Do you know how much they were demanding?" I asked, also keeping it low.

"Not exactly, but a lot. Enough to split three ways and live happily ever after, from the way it sounded." Willie sank down onto the edge of the bathtub, as if his legs wouldn't hold him up anymore.

"Who's the third guy?" I asked, and right about then a horrible suspicion began to seep into my mind. "What's his name?" Had I really recognized his voice?

"I don't remember what they called him. And I don't know what his part is in the kidnapping, but he's in for a share of the money. Bishop, how do you think they're going to *take care of* us?"

"I don't know. But we've got an hour at the most, maybe less, to think of something, before they do whatever they're going to do." I looked wildly around the bathroom for a weapon, for a place to hide, for some kind of miracle. It was just an ordinary bathroom.

"We've got to get out of here, Joe," Willie said. It was the first time I could remember he'd ever called me by my first name.

"I don't think we can," I said slowly.

"Are we giving up, then? We just sit here and wait for them to shoot us, or smuggle our bodies out to the Dumpster?"

Willie was scared, really scared, but I couldn't gloat

over seeing him that way. I was scared, too.

The kidnappers were back in the hallway. "Give me a hand with this stuff," Tedesco said, and I heard something . . . a suitcase? . . . bump against the bathroom door as they passed.

"Maybe we shouldn't leave the kids unguarded. That Bishop kid is inventive," the other man said. "It wouldn't surprise me if he figured out a way to blow up this place and leave a hole in the wall so big the entire police force would come to investigate."

"Ah, they're locked in. What can they do? Here, you take this one . . ." The voices trailed off, still audible but we couldn't make out the words anymore.

Willie swallowed. "He sounded like he knows you."

It couldn't be, I thought. But his voice . . . surely I knew that voice. And I knew who it sounded like. I just didn't want to believe it.

"Maybe he does," I said, sounding hollow. I started pulling open drawers, looking for anything that might be useful. "It sounds a lot like Ernie. Our chauffeur."

Willie blinked, gulped again, and asked, "What are you looking for?"

"A tool. Something to build a bomb. A . . . " My voice trickled off to nothing. In the drawer was a hand mirror, and I stared at it. I couldn't let myself be so scared I couldn't think.

"Can you really build a bomb?" Willie asked hopefully.

"Not with anything I've found so far. I think Mark knows the general principle, but Father said he'd skin him alive if he ever caught him with one of those instruction books again. He found it on a bus."

I reached into the drawer and took out the mirror. "This one's smaller than the mirror on the medicine chest, but maybe it will work."

"For what?" Willie trailed me back to the bedroom window, depending on me to come up with an idea.

"Maybe I can attract attention from the building across the street. Let's find out."

I held up the mirror and tried twisting it up and down, back and forth, trying to pick up enough light with it to flash into one of those apartment windows across the narrow street.

The result was so pale I could barely make out the flashes. Nobody in the windows—the old lady, the guy at the computer, the man watching TV—noticed a thing.

"It's not bright enough," Willie said.

"No. It's not. I need something to produce more light." My mind was racing, already counting those few remaining minutes before our captors decided to *deal with* us. Mom said once she thought I lived 90 percent of my life inside my head, oblivious to what was going on in the real world. Well, it was time it paid off. My life—*our* lives—might depend on it.

"I read something once," I mused as the memory came back. "About Thomas Edison, a biography. I think it was him. His mother needed an operation. A long time ago, you know, before electricity was common. If I remember right, it was an emergency, and the doctor had to perform the surgery there in her house, on the kitchen table. It was night, and I guess they had kerosene lamps, but they didn't give enough light so he could see very well. So Edison, if it was him, got all the mirrors he could find, and grouped them behind the lamps, and it made twice as much light as the lamps alone. Take the shade off that lamp beside the bed, and off the floor lamp, too, and bring them over here . . . "

It seemed perfectly natural to give orders to Willie, and he followed them without hesitation. It wasn't Willie I was afraid of any longer, and he'd forgotten we'd been enemies only yesterday.

"A flashlight would be easier," he complained as he positioned the floor lamp beside me. "What'll I put the small lamp on? Maybe I can slide the nightstand over by the window."

"Since we don't have a flashlight, this'll have to do." We plugged the two lamps in, and then I flipped the mirror around so it picked up the extra light and flashed it out across the darkness.

"You know Morse code, or what?" Willie asked.

"Yeah. I don't know if anybody else does, but almost everybody recognizes a distress signal, don't they? SOS . . . dot-dot-dot, dash-dash-dash, dot-dot-dot."

The signal flashed on the building facing us was still not as bright as I'd have liked, though it was a little bit brighter. I concentrated on the guy with the computer, but he was so absorbed in whatever was on his screen that he didn't notice when the light was focused on him. I repeated the pattern for a minute or so, wondering how he could ignore it.

Finally he got up and moved away from the window.

I sighed in frustration, shifting my weight so that I moved my foot. I looked down, then, because I had stepped on something.

A spoon. I retrieved it and held it up.

"Oh, I must have dropped that when they let me have some ice cream," Willie said. "It's not much of a tool, is it?"

"A table knife would be better. Maybe this would work, though." I set the mirror aside and walked over to the door to look at it closely. "You ever take a door off its hinges?"

"No. What good would that do, anyway? It's still locked."

"True. But I've read about doing this, and I saw my uncle do it once. If we can pry out that rod that drops in from the top of the hinge, we might be able to work the door enough to break it off at the lock, enough so we could squeeze out the crack and get to a phone. Here, you try that, like this, see? And I'll keep trying Morse code at the window."

"The spoon's not really thin enough," Willie grunted after his first attempt.

I picked up the mirror again, pausing to look around one more time. "Is that a closet over there? Are there any wire hangers in it? Maybe one of them would have a section thin enough to fit in that crack. Once the bolt starts to loosen even a little bit, you could get the edge of the spoon under it."

"Okay. I'll try that," Willie agreed.

While he worked on the door, I went through the whole pattern of sending signals across the street, blinking my SOS at the man watching TV. Again, he wasn't aware of anything but his program.

I couldn't help thinking how quickly the time was passing. Half an hour, Tedesco had said. An hour, tops. Studen was out now, picking up the ransom.

"Maybe the police have laid a trap for him," I thought aloud. "Maybe when Studen goes to pick up the ransom money, they'll be waiting for him and arrest him."

"If that happened, do you think he'd confess? And lead them back here?" Willie speculated. "Or would Tedesco and this other guy, your chauffeur, Ernie, split and run if they knew Studen had been arrested?"

"I doubt if they can afford to go anywhere until they get the ransom. Only a week ago Ernie was talking about how expensive it is to take Alice out. She's his girlfriend. He likes to take her to his mother's for dinner because it doesn't cost him anything." I gave up on the TV watcher and angled the mirror so it would reflect into the window of the old lady working the puzzle. "Without money, they can't fly to Mexico or South America or wherever they're planning to go."

I heard Willie swallow. "So do you suppose they have to kill us, so we can't tell what we know about them?"

I didn't answer that. I didn't know, and I didn't want to think about it. I didn't want Ernie to be part of the conspiracy, either, but several things were coming back to me.

It had never occurred to me that Ernie was mixed up in any of this. Now it struck me that he'd kept me from calling the police—something had happened to the cellular he kept in the car, he said—and he didn't kid along with my story the way he usually did with stuff I made up. Instead he'd refused to take me seriously and kept me from reporting the kidnapping as long as he could.

I hadn't thought to look at our car when I got out of it, to see if it had marks from an accident. Ernie said he'd been late on Friday afternoon to pick me up because of a fender bender, yet certainly there hadn't been any obvious damage to the car. I'd been so busy thinking about the kidnapping I never thought that anybody I knew might be mixed up in it.

Ernie hadn't wanted to stop anywhere so I could use a public telephone to call the police. And I'd blabbed about everything, so Ernie and the others had known all the time that I could identify Tedesco. And the car. And he must have known while we were out in the alley that it was the kidnap car. Why had it been there? Not waiting to run over me, because I wouldn't normally have been out there. But maybe because the driver wanted to talk to Ernie about something?

It began to make sense that Ernie was one of the conspirators. Ernie and Tedesco, another chauffeur, and the man called Studen, who had worked for Mr. Zoulas, could easily have gotten acquainted here in the building or in the back alley. They all wanted more money than they got paid for their jobs.

So they decided to try kidnapping. A kid like Willie whose dad could pay a big ransom. What if they'd snatched me, instead?

I didn't want to think about that. One of the men, maybe Ernie, had caused a minor accident with the Groveses' car, so that chauffeur couldn't pick up Willie from school before the kidnappers got there. That made Ernie late getting *me*. He couldn't have known that I'd see the kidnapping, but he could have realized I had when I came running out all excited. He'd had time then to stuff the phone out of sight under the seat so I couldn't use it. Then he'd stalled as long as possible, to let his cohorts get Willie away. And when we came out into the alley, Ernie had pretended he was going to investigate the car when I recognized it, and was as surprised as we were when the car nearly ran over all of us. They didn't know Pink and I would come out the back way, so they couldn't have planned that part.

It made me dizzy thinking about it.

I flipped out the SOS over and over again on the old lady's window. She glanced up once, and my heart leaped, but then she turned back to her puzzle.

Ernie knew about the police artist and the sketch that looked so much like Tedesco. He'd known everything I knew, the whole time. No wonder he'd maneuvered so slowly around the block when Pink spotted the kidnapper in front of the video store; he didn't *want* to catch up to him.

So he'd told Tedesco I was on to him, and the other kidnapper knew what I looked like, either because he'd seen me in the alley or Ernie had described me.

It must have been a shock, finding me in the same elevator with them. Studen was used to using the main elevator, and nobody would be surprised to see him coming in the front door. The doorman had accepted Tedesco as Studen's visitor and let them go up; he wouldn't know Willie had been kidnapped and hidden away in Mr. Zoulas's apartment.

Again the old lady looked up, this time with annoyance, and I concentrated desperately on sending my call for help. The light danced across her face.

Please, please, I begged silently. Figure it out, lady. You must know an SOS when you see one.

She stood up suddenly, and I thought we'd done it.

And then she reached up and pulled down the shade.

Willie was watching, and the significance of this didn't get past him. He hissed a mild curse word under his breath.

I scanned the opposite building, wondering if it was worthwhile to try any other windows. I couldn't see into any of the others very well, and most of them were not lighted.

More in desperation than in any real hope of results, I did my SOS on several of the darkened windows on the floor across that would be just above us.

"Hey," Willie said suddenly. "I think it gave a little bit with the end of this hanger."

"Will the spoon fit in the crack now?" I swung around to watch.

"Yeah, just barely. Joe, I think it's loosening up!"

And then he went rigid, forgetting to pry on the bolt in the top hinge.

"They're back," he said.

Chapter Fourteen

One of them was laughing.

I joined Willie at the door to listen as they came closer to us, on the way to haul out more luggage, I guessed.

"Nobody'll recognize you now," Ernie said.

"I can't wait to be out of here," Tedesco responded sourly. "One more load, and we're set to go. I wish we dared to take Mrs. Civen's car to get out of the city, but I don't want to touch it again. That kid and his big mouth. Why didn't you strangle him while you had a chance?"

"I didn't think I'd have to. If you hadn't been stupid enough to come in the front door and up in the same elevator with him, he'd never have known you were in the building. There was no point in shutting him up after he described you to the cops. By that time the damage was done. If you weren't dumb enough to leave fingerprints in either the car or that junker taxi you swiped, there's no reason to think they'll catch up with you. If you're telling the truth about not having any prints on file."

"I told you, I don't have a record. Come on, grab the last load and let's get it done. The minute Studen gets back with the money, we're out of here, fast."

Their voices faded briefly, then we heard them go past us again.

Willie cautiously inserted the tip of the spoon under the head of the bolt in the hinge and applied leverage. I thought it gave a little.

"When they're gone, I think we can get it out," I whispered.

Beyond the door, the phone rang. We heard somebody swear, and the ringing was cut off.

Once more the spoken words were too muffled to make out. A few moments later the key scrabbled in the lock and Willie and I had trouble moving back before the door was thrown open.

It was Tedesco, and he looked furious. For a few seconds I didn't even recognize him. He was wearing a red and gold kerchief around his head, like a pirate or a gypsy, with big gold hoops hanging from both ears, a jumble of gold chains around his neck, an open-necked red and black shirt, and a multicolor vest that was practically blinding.

People would look at him, but they weren't likely to spot much similarity to the guy in the police sketch, even if they'd seen it. His face didn't even look the same shape.

He shoved us ahead of him toward the bed. "Sit down," he ordered brusquely, and we sank down obediently.

He bent and plugged in the telephone he was carrying, then handed the receiver to Willie. "Talk into it," he snapped.

Willie, bewildered, took the phone. "Hello?" he said cautiously. Then, with delight and relief sweeping over his face, he cried, "Dad? Did you pay the ransom yet?"

"That's enough," Tedesco snarled, and snatched the phone away from him to speak into it himself. "There. You heard the kid. He's alive and well. Now hand over the money to my partner and stay where you are for an hour."

He slapped the receiver back into its cradle, hanging up, and jerked the cord out of the phone jack in the wall. He stalked past us, out the doorway, and the key scraped in the lock as if for a final time.

I guess we were both paralyzed for a minute or so. And then I looked up and saw that the bolt in the hinge had been forced upward, ever so slightly, and there was no further sound out in the apartment.

Willie was off the bed and back at his post, working that spoon tip for all it was worth. My mouth was dry. When he got tired, I took a turn prying up on the bolt.

We didn't talk. We both knew that it was important to get the bolt out, and then the one out of the lower hinge, before the kidnappers came back.

How long did we have? Ten minutes? Less? Maybe only five.

The hinge came loose with a screeching sound, and we laughed breathlessly as our eyes met.

"Now the other one," Willie said, and we started the process all over again.

I'd imagined circumstances like this many times: escaping from captors, improvising tools, outwitting thugs. I was always the hero, usually rescuing someone else, and I was always brilliant.

This time it was myself I needed to rescue, along with Willie, who had until a short time ago been my worst enemy, and I was feeling far less brilliant than I'd always thought I was. I'd read about things like sending SOS signals with mirrors and taking doors off hinges, but I wasn't at all sure they would really work.

The bottom bolt was stiffer, and I felt sweat breaking out under my arms and down my back. We both worked on the bolt on opposite sides, me prying with the spoon, Willie working with the coat hanger.

And then it came free, sending Willie sprawling backward from his squatting position, me nursing a lip where the bolt clipped me when it came free.

Willie gasped for breath. "Now what? Will the lock hold?"

"Let's find out," I said. I stuck the handle of the spoon into the crack along the back of the door and pried.

Willie was right alongside of me, getting the ends of all his fingers into the widening crack. I dropped the spoon and grabbed the edge of the door, and we both pulled.

For a moment it resisted our efforts, and then we heard it beginning to splinter. We both grew red in the face, pulling for all we were worth. Finally Willie reached out for one of the books in the case beside him and crammed it into the crack.

"Ahh! My fingers are breaking off! I gotta rest," he said, breathing heavily.

I rested, too, now that the book kept the door from going back into place; my fingertips were stinging. "Is there anything around we could use for a lever to make it open wider?"

"The mirror handle?" Willie asked. We stuck the handle into the crack, but it was plastic, and it snapped off as soon as we pushed against it.

I looked around, then dove for the bed, pushing the mattress and springs sideways onto the floor. "There're usually metal bed rails to support the springs," I said, and sure enough, there they were. It only took us a few seconds to get one of them loose, and though we made some noise, nobody came.

Now, to get the end of the rail into that crack, which still wasn't quite wide enough for us to get out.

We pulled and twisted, and I rammed the rail into the opening.

When we both pushed on our new lever, the door splintered all the way, breaking a strip off the edge of it. We repositioned the bed rail, and tried again. This time the entire lock broke out of the door.

We were free.

Well, free of the bedroom.

We didn't look back.

We raced toward the front door, only to find that it, too, was locked. They must have used a key, and we didn't have one.

"They went down the service elevator to the alley,"

Willie said, licking his lips apprehensively. "If we go down that way, we'll run into them coming back."

"Nine-one-one, then," I said, and looked around for the phone.

I was halfway across the room when the voice stopped me in my tracks.

"Well, kid, looks like you got yourself a genuine adventure this time," Ernie said.

My heart seemed to stop. My mouth went so dry that for a few moments I couldn't speak.

I hadn't been mistaken. Ernie, the man I had considered a friend as well as my father's employee, had betrayed me. I was confused and hurt and angry.

I'd never before thought about what a big man Ernie was. There was no chance Willie and I could handle him by ourselves. We were at his mercy.

Sounds came from the area where the service elevator opened into the utility area. All three of us glanced in that direction, paralyzed until Tedesco in his garish outfit emerged from the rear hallway.

He stopped, staring at us.

"I told you this kid was a slick little sucker," Ernie said. "They got out of the bedroom and were heading for the phone. Lucky I heard them working on that door and stuck around."

Tedesco swore. His face was so mean I wouldn't have been surprised if he'd whipped out a gun and shot us right then.

"So what do we do with the brats now?" His tone implied that whatever it was, it would be unpleasant.

"If my dad's paid the ransom, aren't you going to let us go?" Willie demanded. And then, as even he realized how naive that sounded, his face began to get red.

They didn't answer that, and I fought against the tremors that started in the pit of my stomach and traveled down my legs. Imaginary heroic adventures had always been entertaining, but a real one like this was no fun at all.

Tedesco had taken two steps toward Willie, the closest to him, when the doorbell rang.

It was like playing statues when we were little kids. Everybody froze.

Ernie finally wet his lips. "That can't be Studen already."

The bell rang again, and this time someone was keeping a finger on it so the sound buzzed through the apartment.

"Police! Open up!"

The deep male voice sent a bigger tremor through me, and I nearly fell down. A glance at Willie suggested he was about to collapse, too.

Tedesco jerked convulsively and swore again. "Come on, let's get out of here," he said, and turned toward the elevator that had just brought him up from the alley.

"Police! Open up!" the command came again, more urgently this time.

A moment later, as both Tedesco and Ernie headed away from Willie and me, something hit the front door hard, then again. This time the lock splintered—the second time in a few minutes that I'd seen it happen—and the door was knocked back against the wall.

"They went that way," Willie gulped, gesturing, and two men with drawn guns ran past us.

I stumbled backward, falling onto a couch, and Willie folded up beside me.

One of the men in plainclothes who had followed the uniformed officers through the doorway was Detective O'Hara. He glanced in our direction with a question. "You kids all right?"

We nodded, unable to speak, and he followed the officers with the guns.

It took a few minutes to get things sorted out. I didn't care how long it took. There were cops all over the place, and nobody was going to shoot us and throw us in the Dumpster.

"I think I need to go to the bathroom," Willie said, and I got up with him.

"Me, too."

By the time we got back to the living room, Detective O'Hara had returned. There was no sign of Ernie and Tedesco. Willie cleared his throat. "I think they had a car in the alley," he said.

The hint of a smile touched the detective's lips. "Our men were waiting for them."

It was my turn to clear my throat. "Can I call my father?"

"We want to keep the phone open right now. We'll let your families know you're both all right."

"Did my dad pay the ransom? Did they get away with it?" Willie asked.

Before, the police hadn't answered any questions.

Now O'Hara was more cooperative. "We think he paid it. There's an officer waiting for him to come home. In the meantime we'll wait for the one who picked up the money. Do you know who he is?"

"His name's Studen," Willie blurted. "He's a secretary for the man who lives here. Mr. Zoulas. *He's* in Paris right now."

I finally was beginning to get my wind again. "How did you know where to find us?"

This time there was definitely a small smile. "We had two phone calls from tenants in the apartment house across the street. They'd seen SOS signals coming from here. Your family had called earlier to say you'd disappeared while running an errand to another apartment in the building, and they were afraid there might be a connection with the kidnapping of Willie Groves. Then they called back five minutes after we heard from the neighbors about the SOS signals. Your brother Mark had noticed the flickering lights against the opposite building. He didn't remember any Morse code, but he thought your sister might, so he called her to look out, too. She recognized the distress signal. Said you used to send secret messages in code. She couldn't tell which apartment the signals were coming from, but the neighbors had pinpointed it exactly by counting windows."

"I bet it ruined my parents' party," I said, remembering. "Is my father mad?"

"I suspect he'll be more relieved than anything else," Detective O'Hara said. "He's been quite concerned about your safety."

"When can we go home?" Willie wanted to know.

"We'd prefer that you sit here, quietly, for a short time," he told us.

He turned and left us there, consulting in low voices with the other officers in the apartment. Two men were attempting repair of the door, putting it back in place, even though it could no longer be locked.

"They're waiting for Studen to come back," Willie said in a low tone. "They don't want to tie up the elevator getting us out of here. Or the phone, in case he calls."

"Yeah. Maybe they'll get the money back."

"I hope so. Otherwise my dad's never going to let me forget it," Willie muttered. "Hey, these guys are all regular police, aren't they? Don't they usually call in the FBI for a kidnapping?"

"Yeah. Usually. I guess we'll find out, sooner or later." I wanted to go home. I was proud of Sophie, and even Mark, for noticing my light signals. And the people I'd thought were ignoring them had not only noticed but they'd called the authorities. Thank you, God, I thought.

There was a sudden, intense silence around us, and Willie and I fell silent, too, without anybody telling us to. A moment later we heard a key in the lock.

Studen must have realized immediately that something was wrong. We heard his startled exclamation, watched the officers get the door out of the way and pour into the hallway, heard the sounds of a struggle as Studen tried for the elevator.

Detective O'Hara seemed to be in charge, but he wasn't

at all excited. I guess he'd already given orders for more officers to be waiting down in the lobby in case Studen and the ransom escaped the men waiting for him here or in the alley.

And that was the end of it. We were free, and neither Willie nor I had a scratch except what we got squeezing out of that bedroom past a broken door.

Nobody was mad at me. Sophie hugged me, and even Mark slapped me on the shoulder the way he did with his buddies.

When Sophie and Mark went to tell Father about the signal lights, they'd both been positive I was responsible for them. Father called the police immediately, then explained to Mom that something urgent had come up. He asked her to fill in for him at the party until he'd taken care of it. She was exasperated with business that had to be taken care of on a Saturday night, but so busy herself she didn't realize at the time that there was something seriously wrong. So the party wasn't ruined after all, though when I got home and we told her, she broke down and cried.

When that was explained to the guests, they thought it was the most excitingly unique party they'd ever attended. When everything appeared in the papers and on TV, they were gratified to have been involved. Even if they didn't know about it until it was all over.

Mr. Groves got the ransom money back. Ernie and Studen and Tedesco eventually had a trial that was in all the papers and on TV. Then they went to jail for quite a long time. Mr. Zoulas was appalled that the conspirators had used his apartment for a headquarters, and of course he had to hire a new secretary.

Mrs. Civen was equally appalled that her chauffeur had used her car and been a party to a kidnapping. The insignia on the doors of her New Yorker had been a gift from her son, who had it made especially for her to look like a royal emblem. That was because her kids referred to as "The Queen," and called her "Your Highness," in fun.

Willie thought we should take a few days off from school the next week to recover from our ordeal, and I'd have been willing. But none of our parents agreed, so we were back in St. Bart's on Monday.

Before our first class I came up behind Willie in the hallway. He was telling a bunch of kids about being kidnapped, gesturing vigorously with his hands. He flipped one of them backward, quite hard, and smacked me in the nose.

It hurt. I put up a hand toward the pain, and brought it away bloody.

Willie spun around and stared at me in dismay. "Oh, no! Not again!" he cried.

My eyes were watering from the pain. I hoped none of the guys thought I was crying.

"Boys." The stern voice was Mr. Giacomo's. "You know there are rules against fighting. I'll see you both in my office after school."

"We weren't fighting," Willie said hastily. "It was an accident. Bishop just got in my way. You know how clumsy he is, sir."

"It's true," Pink said. "They weren't fighting, sir."

Mr. Giacomo scrutinized our faces. "You can explain it to me after school," he said, and went on down the hall.

I spoke in a muffled way through the hand over my nose.

"You're a natural born troublemaker, Groves," I told Willie.

For a moment there was tension in the circle of boys surrounding us. Then Willie said in resignation, "Ain't it the truth."

Everybody exploded in relieved laughter, and Willie threw an arm around my shoulders. "Come on, Bishop, let's find a wet paper towel before you bleed all over your science book."

And that was the only time in my life that I got involved in a kidnapping, and the last time I had a bloody nose.